Santa Paws, Our Hero

Don't miss these other thrilling books in the
Santa Paws series:

SANTA PAWS

THE RETURN OF SANTA PAWS

SANTA PAWS, COME HOME

SANTA PAWS TO THE RESCUE

Santa Paws, Our Hero

by Nicholas Edwards

AN
APPLE
PAPERBACK

SCHOLASTIC INC.

New York   Toronto   London   Auckland   Sydney
Mexico City   New Delhi   Hong Kong   Buenos Aires

ISBN 0-439-37283-6

Cover illustration by Paul Bachem
Designed by Jennifer Rinaldi

12 11 10 9 8 7 6 5 4 3 2   2 3 4 5 6 7/0

Printed in the U.S.A.   40

First Scholastic printing, October 2002

SANTA PAWS, OUR HERO

For the real Dr. K.
Thanks for everything!

1

The dog was a little bit confused. Sometimes, when he went places with his family, a lot of people would gather around and clap their hands, or flash bright lights in his eyes. Other times, the people would wait in a long line and take turns shaking paws with him! He thought it was really strange.

It was the week before Christmas, and there were children everywhere he looked. He liked children — a lot! — so, that was okay. He was sitting on top of a large wooden sleigh, which gave him a great view of the entire mall. It made him feel tall, too. There was a soft red blanket spread across the bench seat, and he was very comfortable. The children would climb up next to him, one at a time, and then talk, and talk, and *talk*. He wasn't always sure what they were saying, but he would watch them intently, and wag his tail the whole time.

His family was standing right nearby, and that

made him happy. He loved his family! He had lived with the Callahans for so long now, that he almost couldn't remember anymore what it was like to be a lonely stray. But he never, ever forgot how lucky he was to have such a wonderful home.

Mrs. Callahan was over by the escalators, drinking a cup of freshly-ground coffee from Jorge's Perk-and-Run, and talking to Mrs. Petronio, the manager of the Oceanport Community Mall. Gregory, who was in the ninth grade, was pacing around in front of the huge "What Holiday Does *Your* Family Celebrate?" display. He was holding a plastic container of special dried liver treats, and every so often, he came over and gave the dog a few to eat. Milk-Bones were the dog's very favorite, but the liver bits were delicious, too. Actually, in the dog's opinion, *all* food was delicious.

In the meantime, Patricia was leaning on the edge of the fountain, with her face shaded by her Bruins cap and bright yellow sunglasses. She was fifteen and had just started high school this year. Since that made her even more cool than she had been in junior high, she was pretending that she hadn't come to the *mall*, with her *family*, *voluntarily*, on a Saturday afternoon.

Mr. Callahan had stayed home to work on his new book, along with the dog's two cat friends, Abigail and Evelyn. But, the dog was pretty sure that the cats weren't working. Mostly, they spent their time *sleeping*.

A news crew from one of the local television stations was behind a velvet rope in the designated press area, in front of the sleigh. Several print reporters and photographers from the newspapers and a North Shore monthly magazine had also come. They were all hoping that this would turn out to be an exciting event, but even if it didn't, it would still be a nice holiday feature story.

A man boosted his little girl Barbara up into the sleigh, and she sat down right next to the dog.

"Hi, Santa Paws!" she said, so excited that she was almost shouting. "Merry Christmas, Santa Paws!"

The dog lifted his paw, and Barbara shook it.

"Did you get your hat at the North Pole?" she asked.

The dog cocked his head to one side, which made his Santa hat flop over. It felt a little odd on his head, but since Gregory had put it on him earlier, he figured that there must be some good reason for him to be wearing it. So he hadn't tried to take it off, even when it got in his way.

"I have been very, very good this year, Santa Paws," Barbara said.

She thought he was good. Yay! What a nice little girl. The dog wagged his tail.

As Barbara told Santa Paws her long Christmas wish list, Gregory walked over to the fountain. He and his sister looked almost like twins, with the same dark brown hair and extremely blue eyes. But even though he was a year younger, Gregory was more than six inches taller — and getting very muscular. His dream was to play on the football team when he went to high school next year, and it was starting to seem much more plausible than it had before he started growing so quickly. Patricia, on the other hand, was still very short and thin. To her endless annoyance, this often made people think she was younger than she was. She found it unspeakably irritating to look as though she could still be in junior high. Gregory assumed that was why she usually acted about *forty*.

"You think he's getting tired?" he asked Patricia.

Patricia glanced up at the sleigh. "He seems all right. Besides, you know Mom's going to pull the plug soon, anyway."

Gregory nodded. Mrs. Callahan was very strict about how long any events like this could last — and she had been checking her watch regularly during this particular session. Santa Paws was famous all over New England, and maybe even all over *America*, so there were always lots of requests for him to make public appearances.

The whole family had discussed whether they ought to accept *any* of the invitations — or if he should just be allowed to spend as much time as possible being a normal dog.

The only problem was that Santa Paws wasn't a normal dog. No one knew why, but ever since he was a puppy, he had been saving people, and pets, from all sorts of accidents and other predicaments. He seemed to have a special instinct for sensing trouble — and a knack for fixing whatever went wrong. Some people thought he was magic, while others assumed that he was unusually smart. There was even a theory floating around the Internet that he wasn't just one dog, but a *team* of specially-bred German shepherd mixes, who had been trained by a top-secret government agency to perform rescue missions throughout the land. In any case, for better or worse, he was a full-time hero.

"What about the hat?" Gregory asked. "Do you think he hates the hat?"

"*I* hate the hat," Patricia said. "It's totally not dignified."

Gregory looked worried. Was being dignified important to Santa Paws? Or did he not care? It seemed like he didn't really mind wearing it, but maybe he was just being a good sport. Santa Paws was nothing if not agreeable.

Seeing his expression, Patricia took pity on

5

him. "Don't worry, Greg, he's fine. I think he likes doing this stuff. And it's making all those kids really happy."

Gregory kept frowning. "Maybe I should bring him some more treats."

"Well, he'll *definitely* like that," Patricia said.

A little boy named Simon was talking to Santa Paws now. He was so overjoyed to be next to the famous dog that he couldn't stop bouncing around. Suddenly, he lost his balance and started to topple out of the sleigh head-first. His mother screamed and tried to run forward to catch him. He was going to fall and hurt himself!

Just at that second, Santa Paws lunged over and caught the back of the boy's jacket in his teeth. He pulled the boy back into the sleigh, and set him carefully on the blanket. It had all happened so quickly that Simon hadn't even had time to start crying yet. Now, as his mother rushed over to hug him, the little boy's eyes filled with tears.

"Did you see, Mommy?" Simon asked. "Santa Paws saved me!"

"Yes," his mother answered, still trying to recover her composure. Her son had given her quite a scare. "I certainly did." She turned to the dog and gave him a pat. "Thank you so much, Santa Paws."

The dog wagged his tail. Then, he saw Gregory

hurrying over with the liver treats. Yay! Snack-time!

"He's really something, isn't he," Mrs. Petro-nio, the mall manager, said to Mrs. Callahan.

"That about covers it," Mrs. Callahan agreed. Over the years, she had learned to accept the fact that when it came to rescuing people, Santa Paws just couldn't help himself. And since he had saved *her* life the previous Christmas, when her car crashed on an icy, deserted road, she was more than a little grateful to him.

After telling Santa Paws how good he was and feeding him a small handful of treats, Gregory stepped aside to let some more children have a chance to sit up in the sleigh for a minute. He decided to stay close by, though, so that he could be in position to give Santa Paws some fast back-up, if another little kid decided to take a tumble.

Over in the press area, the reporters were jot-ting down notes, and the photographers were snapping photos, while the news camera filmed the dramatic episode.

"Boy, is he good copy," one reporter said to an-other, who nodded enthusiastically. There was no such thing as a dull day when it came to cover-ing Santa Paws!

The line of children seemed to get longer and longer, stretching all the way down to the Light-house Bookshop. After Mrs. Callahan tapped her watch significantly, the mall manager stepped forward to announce that Santa Paws would only be in the sleigh for another ten minutes. After that, one of Santa Claus's human helpers was going to come and take over for him. The children near the back of the line looked disappointed, until Mrs. Petronio explained that Santa Paws was getting tired and needed to save his energy for his next heroic act.

"Save his energy for his next *nap*, more likely," Patricia muttered to Gregory.

Gregory laughed, since Santa Paws loved naps almost as much as he loved food.

"Lots of times I'm kind of bad," a little boy named Butch was telling Santa Paws earnestly. "I never clean up my room. Do you think I'll still get presents?"

Bad? The dog really didn't like the word "bad," and his posture stiffened.

"I'm going to be good for the whole rest of the year," Butch promised. "I'll even help with the dishes tonight. I might set the table, too."

Hearing the word "good," the dog relaxed. *That* was what he liked to hear.

Seeing that Santa Paws was pleased now, Butch smiled and got off the sleigh. Maybe he would get lots of gifts, after all!

During the next child's long explanation of the various types of Barbie models, and why some were great, and others were just too silly, Santa

Paws suddenly stood up and sniffed the air. Something was bothering him, but he wasn't sure what it was yet.

Down in the Oceanport Entertainment Emporium, two boys from the high school had decided to take advantage of the holiday crowds and shoplift some DVDs. They were twins named Luke and Rich Crandall, and they were well-known in Oceanport for being terrible troublemakers. Actually, the Crandalls were old enough to be in college, but they had each stayed back twice. So far. Since they almost never went to class or studied, they usually flunked all of their courses.

"Think we've got enough?" Luke asked his brother, as they each stuffed DVDs into their zipped ski jackets.

Rich looked down at his bulging jacket. "Yeah. Let's get out of here."

Luke nodded, and they ambled toward the exit, doing their best to look casual.

In the meantime, Santa Paws leaped out of the sleigh and raced down the mall. The television news crew chased after him, in the hopes of getting some good footage. As Luke and Rich started to leave the store, the security tags on the DVDs triggered a loud alarm. The boys had expected this, but knew that they could outrun any of the mall's security officers, so they weren't concerned.

9

What they *didn't* expect was to find Santa Paws standing right outside the store, waiting for them! They were so surprised that they raised their hands defensively, and the DVDs spilled out of their jackets.

The dog growled low in his throat. He had run into the Crandalls many times before, and they were always misbehaving.

"Why does this stupid dog show up every time we try to have some fun?" Luke asked his brother, who shrugged.

Then, the twins tried to dodge past him, but the dog kept growling and backed them into the store. Three mall security guards hustled over to take charge of the situation. The news crew and reporters were only steps behind them.

Santa Paws yawned and sat down to scratch an itch near his shoulder. He was getting very hungry and he wondered if he and his family would be going home to eat supper soon. And he'd like to go play with his cat friends for a while, too.

Rich looked pleased when he saw all of the cameras. "Oh, wow. Are we going to be on television?"

"Are you juveniles?" the on-air reporter asked.

"Not since October," Luke said proudly.

The reporter shrugged. "Then, you're going to be on television."

"Cool!" the twins said, and gave each other high fives.

Santa Paws yawned again, and then stood up to stretch. It was warm in the mall, which made him feel a little sleepy. After supper, maybe he would take a nap in front of the fireplace at home. That would be fun!

He saw his family coming over to join him, and wagged his tail.

"Good dog," Gregory said, and bent down to take off his Santa Claus hat.

Santa Paws wagged his tail. It was a nice hat, but *not* wearing it was much better than wearing it.

Most of the reporters gathered around them, with their notepads and tape recorders out, hoping to get a quote from one — or all — of the Callahans.

"Do you think Santa Paws was trying to make a statement about law and order?" one of them asked.

"Yeah, he's running for Congress," Patricia said. "It's part of his platform. Don't you people read the position papers we hand out?"

Mrs. Callahan frowned at her.

"Or maybe not," Patricia said, much more quietly.

The on-air reporter held the microphone near Mrs. Callahan. "Would you care to make a comment, ma'am?"

Mrs. Callahan had an unbreakable policy of *never* speaking to the press about Santa Paws, so she shook her head pleasantly. "No, thank you," she said. "But, happy holidays to you all."

Before any of the reporters could try and question Gregory or Patricia, Mrs. Callahan was already ushering them — and Santa Paws — away. Once they had said good-bye to Mrs. Petronio, Santa Paws barked in a friendly way at the remaining crowd and followed his family toward the main exit.

But he had only made it a few steps before he stopped short. His ears pricked forward, and he stood very alertly. He could sense yet another problem somewhere in the mall, but he couldn't quite pinpoint it.

"Oh, no," Gregory said, when he saw the dog snap to attention.

Mrs. Callahan didn't like the sound of that, and she turned to see what was going on. "What is it?" she asked.

Santa Paws was already galloping away!

2

This time, the dog ran straight to the food court. He could smell smoke, and followed the scent to the Hamburger Habitat, where a small grease fire had broken out on the grill.

The line cook's apron had caught on fire and he was waving his arms around in a complete panic. "Help!" he yelled. "Somebody help me!"

While the two cashiers tried to remember where the fire extinguisher was stored, Santa Paws took charge. He knocked the man down and beat his paws against the front of the man's apron until the flames were out.

Seeing that the cashiers were about to throw water onto the grill, Patricia took it upon herself to vault over the counter.

"Drop that!" she said, with great authority.

The cashiers were startled, but did as they were told. *Instantly.*

Then Patricia covered the fire on the grill with a large metal pan lid. The lack of oxygen swiftly smothered the flames, and the emergency was over. She looked around to make sure that everything else was under control, and then jumped back to the customer's side of the counter.

"Smarty-pants," Gregory said, mostly because he wished that he had thought of doing that before she had.

Patricia grinned. "Yep." She had remembered from a long-ago field trip to the Oceanport Fire Department that you were *never* supposed to put water on a grease fire, because it would just spread the flames. The rules were to try smothering it with a pan lid or baking soda — and to call 911 right away. And while fire extinguishers were great, some types only worked on certain kinds of fires, and if you used the wrong one, you could make a fire much worse.

The mall's fire marshal, Mr. Gustave, had been summoned from his office and he carefully examined the whole area to make sure that the fire was completely out. Mikey, the line cook, was staring down at the scorched remains of his apron, but Santa Paws had saved him from possibly being badly burned.

"Uh, thanks," he said shakily, and reached over to pat Santa Paws on the head.

The dog gave his hand a friendly lick in return.

"Come here, boy," Gregory said, snapping his fingers.

The dog romped over to him, wagging his tail.

Gregory lifted each of his feet up one at a time, checking to make sure that he wasn't injured. One paw looked a little bit blistered, and he showed it to his mother.

"Let's get him right to the vet," Mrs. Callahan said.

Horrified at the thought that the great Santa Paws might be hurt, the crowd parted respectfully to let them pass. The dog was barely even limping, but everyone was still very concerned.

Mrs. Callahan called ahead on her cellphone, and Dr. Kasanofsky kept his veterinary office open late just for them. After a full examination, he said that Santa Paws was just fine, except for the little blister. He gave them some prescription ointment, and advised them to keep his paw as clean and dry as possible while it healed.

"I know it's especially hard at this time of year," Dr. Kasanofsky said, "But if you can, try to get him to cut down on his rescues for a few days, too."

They all — including Dr. Kasanofsky — looked at one another, knowing how impossible that was going to be.

"Well," Gregory said finally. "We'll *definitely* keep his paw clean."

When they got home, the house was almost completely dark, even though the sun had gone down a couple of hours earlier.

"I hope the power didn't go out again," Gregory said.

Mrs. Callahan shook her head. "I think the den light is on. Your father's probably busy working, and forgot to turn the rest of the lights on."

When they walked into the kitchen, there was no sign that anyone had been in the room for hours, and — more to the point — dinner had not been started, even though it was Mr. Callahan's turn to cook. However, there *was* the familiar sound of Frank Sinatra's singing pouring out from the den.

"Will you go see if you can dislodge him, Patricia?" Mrs. Callahan asked, as she opened the refrigerator to try and figure out what to make for supper.

"Okay," Patricia said, "but if he's singing along, I'm coming right back."

Mr. Callahan only accompanied Frank Sinatra when he had terrible writer's block — and was in an equally bad mood. Afterward, he would insist that he had been doing no such thing, because it would be just criminal to interfere in any way with the greatest singer who had ever lived. "Yeah, okay, whatever you say," the rest of the family would answer.

The family cats, Evelyn and Abigail, came into the kitchen to greet them. Evelyn took her time, but Abigail raced in at top-speed. Then she abruptly stopped, yawned, and stretched up to scratch her claws against one of the kitchen table legs.

"Please don't do that, Abigail," Mrs. Callahan said mildly. "One of these days, that table's going to collapse."

Abigail, as usual, ignored this and kept scratching away. She was very pleased by the amount of damage she had managed to inflict upon the wood during the two years that she had lived with the Callahans. Like Santa Paws, she had been a stray. During the awful Christmas that Santa Paws got stolen, he had come across the mischievous black kitten while he was trying to make his way back to Oceanport. Naturally, Abigail had decided to accompany him for the rest of the long journey — no matter *what* Santa Paws thought about the idea.

Evelyn was an older tiger cat who thought that both Abigail and Santa Paws were reasonably entertaining, but much too noisy. She considered herself the primary pet in the household, and treated the other two accordingly.

Santa Paws happily greeted both of his cat friends. It was *so good* to see them! Evelyn hissed at him and Abigail whacked him in the side with her paw, but the dog knew that was just their way of saying hello. He gave them a friendly growl back, and used one of his paws to knock Abigail over and roughhouse with her a little.

"Would you please feed them, Gregory?" Mrs. Callahan asked. "That might make them calm down."

Gregory nodded and went to the pantry to get some cans of food. This got all three animals' full attention, and they waited expectantly by their dishes.

While the others were occupied in the kitchen, Patricia paused just outside the den door to listen. Luckily, she could only hear Frank Sinatra, along with his orchestral accompaniment. So, she went into the room to find her father staring at his computer, with both hands completely still, but poised above the keyboard. She wasn't sure what his new book was about, but the fact that he was wearing an official police hat gave her a clue. Mr. Callahan insisted that he wrote much better when he had *props*.

"Hi, Dad," she said.

Mr. Callahan looked up with a certain amount of confusion. "Hi there. You're home early." Then, he checked his watch. "Oh. You're home *late*." He thought about that. "Is it my night to cook?"

Patricia nodded.

"Is your mother out there doing it for me?" he asked.

Patricia nodded.

"Oops," Mr. Callahan said, and got up from his desk. Then he remembered that he was still wearing his police hat and took it off.

"Did Uncle Steve lend you that?" she asked.

Mr. Callahan nodded. "I told him I'd give it back in a couple of weeks." His little brother had been a member of the Oceanport Police Department for almost ten years. He had started off as a patrol officer, but kept taking all of the promotional exams, so he was now a lieutenant.

They headed out to the kitchen, where Mr. Callahan immediately began apologizing for not having gotten dinner ready before they got home. "You know, I *meant* to remember," he kept saying.

Mrs. Callahan had already put a meatloaf and some baked potatoes in the oven, so her only response was to point him in the direction of the salad she had been about to prepare. Mr. Callahan nodded rather meekly, managing to look quite a bit less tall than 6'2". Despite his height, he *never* looked imposing, because his hair was always rumpled and he had a tendency to slouch.

Gregory automatically glanced down at his father's feet and motioned toward Patricia. She looked over, saw that he was wearing fuzzy pink elephant slippers, and laughed quietly. Mr. Callahan almost always forgot to change into regular

19

shoes when he left the house, and they were all so used to it by now that they usually didn't remember to remind him.

The dog had finished his supper, but he was still hungry. Abigail's dish was more than half full, but he knew that if he went over there, she would pounce on him from behind. He took one cautious step toward the dish, and her yellowish-orange eyes gleamed in anticipation. So, he decided to lie down on the rug instead, feeling a little sorry for himself. But then, Patricia came over and started brushing him, and he cheered right up. The brush felt good!

Once dinner was ready and the whole family was sitting at the table, Santa Paws went over to lie on Gregory's feet. Abigail jumped onto the table twice, trying to make a lunge for the meatloaf, but Mr. Callahan was able to intercept her each time. Evelyn had — sensibly — gone off to the couch in the den for a nap.

"I really thought that an afternoon at the mall was going to be pretty boring," Mr. Callahan said, as he tossed the salad. The others had already told him about the way Santa Paws had made repeated rescues, and ended up having to be taken to see Dr. Kasanofsky afterward. "What else does he have scheduled for this week?"

"Well, he's hoping to end world hunger," Patricia said. "And then, after that, he's going to find cures for all kinds of diseases, right, Santa Paws?"

Hearing his name, the dog thumped his tail against the floor.

"He might finish designing those plans to set up a fully-functioning colony on Mars, too," she added.

Gregory ignored all of that. Earlier in the year, he and his mother had gone to some training classes, so that Santa Paws could become a certified pet therapy dog. Many hospitals and places like that were pleased to have animals come visit and try to cheer people up, but even for Santa Paws, there were lots of rules. For one thing, he had had to pass a test, and earn his official Canine Good Citizen certificate! He had also had a full medical check-up, so that the hospital could be sure that his vaccinations were all up-to-date. Anyway, ever since the training sessions, Gregory had kept careful track of each and every appearance Santa Paws made on the calendar in his room. Abigail sometimes came along, too, but not very often. Gregory could always tell if she was in the mood, because she would climb right into her cat carrier if she felt like going. Evelyn had come once, but being at the hospital made her too nervous, so they didn't try to take her again.

"We're supposed to go to the nursing home tomorrow," he said. "And the hospital on Tuesday, after I get out of basketball practice. And then,

you know, it's Christmas Eve, so I figure he'll be
— well — *busy.*"

Patricia and their parents winced at the
thought of what Santa Paws being "busy" could
mean. The possibilities were endless.

"Or not busy at all," Gregory said quickly. "He
might, like, just want to take it easy this year."

"Want to put money on that?" Patricia asked.

Gregory knew a sucker's bet when he heard
one, so he shook his head.

Mrs. Callahan put her fork down. "Since we're
all here, we ought to talk about Christmas some
more. I really think that we should take up Steve
and Emily on their offer."

Aunt Emily had grown up on Beacon Hill in
Boston, and her parents still lived in a big
brownstone on Pinckney Street. Aunt Emily,
Uncle Steve, and their two children, Miranda and
Lucy, were going to spend Christmas there —
and the Callahans, including all three pets, had
been invited to join them.

Gregory and Patricia looked at her doubtfully.

"Why?" Gregory asked. "Won't we feel kind of
— I don't know — homesick?"

"Well, maybe," Mrs. Callahan conceded. "But
I'm really tired of having such stressful holidays.
I think we might be better off just leaving town
for a couple of days."

"The *last* time we went away at Christmas,

our plane crashed," Patricia said. She and Gregory and Santa Paws had been flying in Uncle Steve's private plane, and they had gone down in the middle of the White Mountains in northern New Hampshire. If Santa Paws hadn't led them to safety, for miles — through a blizzard! — none of them would have survived.

"We'd be in the city this time," Mrs. Callahan pointed out. "It would be completely different."

Patricia was going to say something like, "Oh, yeah, nothing *ever* goes wrong in cities," but she changed her mind. "If you want us to go to a city, how about San Francisco?" she suggested. "Or Seattle? If we go to Boston, too many people might recognize Santa Paws and bother him, and all."

Now it was Mr. Callahan's turn to put down his fork. "Since when don't you like Boston, Patricia? Usually you complain that we don't go there *enough*."

"Oh, well, I just — " She stopped to give that some thought. "You're right. Never mind. I think it's a swell idea."

Mrs. Callahan looked at Gregory. "What about you?"

"Well, as long as Santa Paws and the cats can come, I guess it's okay," he said, trying not to sound reluctant. He decided that it would be rude to ask if Aunt Emily's parents had cable, and Internet access, but if they were only going to be there for a couple of days, maybe that wasn't crucial. Maybe.

"If we're going to do it, it should be unanimous," Mrs. Callahan said to her husband.

Mr. Callahan shrugged. "Sounds good to me. When do we leave?"

With that, it was decided.

They were going to spend Christmas in the city!

3

The next morning, Santa Paws had a bath. He didn't like baths, but he knew it meant that he would be going to go visit people later on. And visiting people was fun! They always looked happy when he came into their rooms, and patted him a lot, and gave him treats.

He was a little bit cold when he jumped out of the bathtub, but Patricia wrapped him up in a thick towel. The towel felt good, but he decided to shake the water off instead, spraying drops all over the bathroom. After wiping up the mess, Gregory and Patricia clipped his nails and even brushed his teeth.

"He really is pretty cooperative about all of this," Patricia said, rinsing off the toothbrush. She had used special chicken-flavored dog toothpaste, because Santa Paws seemed to like the taste. Whenever he made pet therapy dog visits, he had to be cleaned up as much as possible, so that no one would worry about germs. He also had a special bandana and harness he wore whenever he was acting in his official Animal-Assisted Therapy dog capacity.

"I kind of think he's *generally* cooperative," Gregory said, and Patricia had to agree.

Today, Abigail was going to come, too, so they had the terrible chore of bathing *her*. She was full of yowling cat complaints the entire time, but actually didn't struggle very much. Mostly, she just seemed to enjoy making noise and splashing a lot. She had never been willing to wear a pet therapy bandana, and a Santa hat was out of the question, but Gregory put one jingle bell on her collar. She also allowed her small harness to be buckled on, so that she could be walked on a leash — if absolutely necessary.

After lunch, Abigail stalled for a while, but then consented to go inside her carrier for the ride over to the Seaside Nursing Home. Her only assignment would be to sit quietly with people, be admired a great deal — and not to bite or scratch anyone. If she deigned to purr, that was a bonus.

Santa Paws and Gregory rode in the backseat with her, while Patricia sat up front with Mr. Callahan. Mrs. Callahan had too many papers to grade — she taught physics at Oceanport High School — and so, she stayed home this time. But she had baked several dozen Christmas cookies, which they were going to give to people at the nursing home.

"Don't forget to keep an eye on the time, Dad," Patricia said. "Mom'll get upset if the animals are there too long."

Mr. Callahan grinned wryly. "This has already been impressed upon me, Patricia. At length."

Patricia grinned back, fairly certain that he wasn't exaggerating.

Right before they got out of the car, the dog leaned his head forward. That way, Gregory could put on his Santa hat. As soon as the dog had seen Gregory stick it in his jacket pocket, he knew that he would be *wearing* it at some point.

They walked inside with Gregory holding Santa Paws's leash, Patricia lugging Abigail's carrier, and Mr. Callahan carrying the box of cookies. Gregory and Patricia really liked visiting Seaside, because their grandparents on their father's side lived up in northern Vermont, so they didn't get to see them often enough. In fact, this Christmas, they were traveling over in the British Isles, so they weren't going to get to see them at all. Their grandparents on their mother's side, unfortunately, weren't around anymore, and Gregory and Patricia — and their mother — missed them very much.

Anyway, they had visited Seaside frequently, so they knew many of the people who lived there. It was like having a whole extra batch of grandparents!

The first person who saw them come in was Mr. Bennington, who was sitting in his wheelchair in the front lobby. He was ninety-nine years old, and liked to pretend that he was the most cranky man alive. He also always insisted that he'd fought in the Civil War *and* the War of 1812. "So, what, you missed the Revolutionary War?" Patricia would ask. Mr. Bennington would chuckle and tell her all about his trip across the Delaware, sitting right behind George Washington in the rowboat.

"What are you people doing here again?" he demanded. "And don't tell me you brought that awful cat."

"Yes, sir," Patricia said, and opened Abigail's carrier door.

Abigail jumped out, looked around, and walked toward Mr. Bennington. Then she stopped just out of his reach, yawned widely, sat down on the floor, and began to wash her face. He leaned over to pat her, and she moved a little bit farther away.

"Cat after my own heart," Mr. Bennington said, trying to not laugh, but unable to help himself.

They stayed at the nursing home for just over an hour, so that the animals wouldn't get too tired. Mr. Callahan ended up in the common room, watching football and eating cookies with a large group of residents. Gregory and Patricia took the animals from room to room, to see who might want visitors. Abigail got bored after about six rooms, and climbed up onto a bed to take a nap. The woman in the bed, Mrs. Kristophe, was delighted to have a cat visitor, because she was recuperating from surgery and had been feeling very lonely.

Santa Paws seemed to take a different strategy with every single person — and Gregory and Patricia knew enough to stay out of his way. If someone seemed afraid of dogs, he would keep his distance and just wave his tail gently. Other people liked a more enthusiastic greeting, and even wanted to be kissed. Some people wanted him to "speak," so he would bark, while others preferred a brief, very quiet visit. Without being told, Santa Paws always seemed to know just what to do.

The first few times Gregory and Patricia made pet therapy visits, they had been kind of nervous. They were sure they wouldn't be able to think of things to say, or know how to make people feel comfortable. It turned out that, more than anything, most people enjoyed talking about pets *they* had owned over the years. How cute they were, the many clever things they would do, and how much they missed each and every one of them. Throughout these conversations, Santa Paws would listen gravely, tilt his head in one direction or another, and sometimes even make little, sympathetic noises.

As they walked down the hall, a man on a cane started to lose his balance. Santa Paws sprang in front of him to block his fall. Once he was sure the man felt more steady, he stepped back.

"Why, thank you, Santa Paws," the man said, and went on his way.

In the next room, Santa Paws started to approach one side of the bed, stopped, and veered over to the other side. Then he put his front paws delicately on the bed rails, so that the woman lying there, Mrs. Osgood, would be able to see him better.

"She had a stroke recently," Mrs. Osgood's son, who was sitting in a visitor's chair, told them. "He's on the wrong side, because she can't move that arm."

Mrs. Osgood was already slowly, shakily, lifting her weakened hand to give Santa Paws a pat.

"Oh," her son said, looking surprised. "Never mind."

The dog wagged his tail at Mrs. Osgood, and moved a few inches away. She reached out again, with great difficulty, but still managed to graze the top of his head with her hand. The dog gave her a little woof of encouragement, and Mrs. Osgood looked pleased.

"You are a good dog," she told him, carefully enunciating each word.

Her speech was a little bit indistinct, but Santa Paws understood completely. His answering woof was very happy. She thought he was good! He thought *she* was good. He was having such a nice time here!

It didn't seem as though patting a dog could be a physical therapy exercise — but it was. Doing repetitive exercises could be a chore, but playing with an animal made it fun. Helping people start to regain their mobility — and confidence — was one of the most important parts of the dog's visits.

Then, it was time to leave, and Abigail had to be roused — reluctantly — from her nap with Mrs. Kristophe. She spent some extra time stretching, and even more time yawning. But finally, she climbed grumpily into her cat carrier. She didn't think it was fair that she had to ride in a carrier, when the dog didn't. All *he* did was wear a seat belt. She would have to swat him a few times later on, to make up for this terrible injustice.

"Boy, not even one miracle today," Patricia said in the car. "Santa Paws is losing his touch."

"He and Abigail made people smile," Mr. Callahan reminded her. "I think that's worth something, don't you?"

Patricia considered that, and then nodded.

So it was.

The next day was Monday, so Gregory, Patricia and Mrs. Callahan all had to go to school. Patricia had spent most of September complaining about how horribly embarrassing it was to attend the same school where her mother was a teacher. Finally, her parents offered to send her to an all-girls' Catholic school where she would have to wear a uniform — and Patricia hadn't mentioned the subject since.

The dog watched unhappily as they all hurried through breakfast and got ready to leave. He wished that they would stay home and keep him company, instead. Why did they go away all the time? It was so sad. He slumped down onto the floor and rested his head mournfully on his paws.

Gregory had his gym bag packed up for basketball practice, as well as his books, and Patricia was lugging her hockey gear and uniform because her high school team had a game after school. Since it was only her first year there, the coach had projected her as a member of the junior varsity when the season began. But, after watching her play — once — the coach had instantly promoted her to the varsity, and she now started every game at left wing.

Gregory preferred football to basketball, but he was still a good enough player to be a member of the starting five at the junior high. Even so, he and his best friend Oscar were counting the days until football tryouts began the following summer. Gregory also did fifty push-ups every night before he went to bed, and another fifty as soon as he woke up in the morning, to help get ready.

They *did* all pat the dog and say good-bye before they left, but they still *left*. Mr. Callahan gave him a Milk-Bone, and he cheered up for a minute. But once the bone was gone, he went back to being miserable.

It wasn't even nine o'clock in the morning, and Mr. Callahan had already been felled by severe writer's block. So he went into the den to lie on the couch and stare up at the ceiling. That fit the dog's mood perfectly, and he stretched out on the floor next to him. All of this sloth appealed to Evelyn, and she curled up on Mr. Callahan's chest, quite content to sleep the rest of the day away.

Abigail was disgusted to see so much resting going on, this early in the morning. She grabbed a doughnut from the plate Mr. Callahan had left on the coffee table. Then she sprawled on the rug to wrestle wildly with the pastry. She fought with it until she was covered with crumbs — and then lost interest in the battered remains. So she positioned herself right next to the dog's head and peered into his face.

The dog woke up to see huge yellow cat eyes looming at him from only an inch or two away, and he yelped with surprise. This also woke up Mr. Callahan and Evelyn, who did their own personal versions of grumbling and complaining before dozing off again.

Amused by having disrupted the communal nap, Abigail decided that she was a little sleepy herself. So she found a basket of freshly washed laundry out in the pantry and burrowed deep inside. It was a fine place to rest — and to shed as much stray fur as possible.

About an hour later, the dog woke up again, feeling much more cheerful. He wandered out to the kitchen and drank enthusiastically from his water bowl. Then he sniffed around the floor for a while, hoping to find a stray Milk-Bone. As he passed the pantry, a black blur of fur flew out of the laundry basket straight at him!

The dog banged into the wall as he tried to get out of the way. It hurt, and he whimpered a couple of times. Abigail landed gracefully on the floor next to him, stared at him, and blinked her eyes a few times. The dog decided that it would be fun to chase her around the house — and so, he did.

They raced through the downstairs rooms, and then Abigail streaked upstairs, with Santa Paws only inches behind her. She led him through each one of the bedrooms, and they left a trail of knocked-over pillows and books on the floor before tearing back downstairs.

Mr. Callahan woke up when he heard the distinctive sound of a Christmas ornament breaking. He got off the couch just in time to see Abigail and Santa Paws gallop through the den at top-speed.

"Hey, now," he said. "Do I see two pets with just a little bit too much energy?"

Santa Paws stopped at once, and looked very guilty. He knew that he had been bad. Was Mr. Callahan angry at him? That would be awful! He sat on the floor with his head hanging down.

Abigail felt no remorse at all, but just in case, she purred sweetly and rubbed against Mr. Callahan's legs.

"Do I look like a soft touch to you?" he asked her.

Abigail purred more loudly.

"I guess that means yes," Mr. Callahan said. He patted her, patted Santa Paws, and then went into the living room to check the Christmas tree for damage.

The tree was still standing, but several ornaments had fallen off and the wrapping was torn on two of the presents. Mr. Callahan rehung the intact ornaments and swept up the broken bits of the one which had shattered. Then, he turned the two gifts over so that the little torn parts wouldn't show.

"Much better," he said, and headed for the kitchen.

The dog followed him, wagging his tail apologetically.

"Why don't you go outside, my little friend, and burn some of that energy off?" Mr. Callahan suggested.

The dog's ears went up. He was going out? It was fun to go out! He waited for Mr. Callahan to open the back door and then dashed into the backyard.

There was no snow, but the ground was hard and frozen underneath his paws. He ran in circles around the yard until he felt tired enough to go back inside. His stomach was growling, so it must be almost lunchtime.

The dog lifted his paw to bang against the back door, but then paused. He felt the hair go up on his back, and knew that somewhere in Oceanport, someone needed his help. He ran to the gate by the driveway and jumped over it without breaking stride.

Once he was in the street, he raised his head to sniff the air. He turned in a slow circle, trying to locate the source of the problem. Once he felt sure of the right direction, he began trotting toward the ocean — and the seawall.

As he moved steadily down Main Street, people waved and called his name and beeped their car horns. The dog wagged his tail, but never strayed from his path. His instincts were telling him to go down to the ocean, and so that's what he was going to do.

He passed through the municipal park, where Oceanport's annual "Festival of Many Lands" holiday extravaganza was set up. Oceanport was an unusually diverse community, and the town liked to pay tribute to each and every one of its cultural traditions during the holidays.

Two men were putting the finishing touches on the jolly *Sinterklass* exhibit, sponsored by the Oceanport Netherlands Appreciation Society. They had just inspected the *Buon Natale* booth, which told about the legend of an elderly lady named *La Befana*, and had been designed by Oceanport's Italian-American League.

"Hey there, Santa Paws," one of them said. "Happy holidays!"

"*Mele Kalikimaka*," the other man added, in perfect Hawaiian. They would be putting some newly-acquired tropical decorations on the tall Norfolk Island pine tree in the *Aloha, Oceanport!* display next.

The dog barked politely, but kept going.

At Ocean Road, he had to wait for several cars to pass before crossing over to the seawall. He lifted his paws up onto the rough stone wall and inhaled several times. All he could smell was the

37

sharp brine of the ocean, and he couldn't hear anything except the choppy waves crashing against the rocks. Everything seemed to be okay, but how could it be? Why would he have felt the need to come down here, otherwise?

He explored the length of the seawall for a hundred feet in both directions. Then, he caught the scent of another dog, and scrambled back up onto the seawall so that he could see better. A small rust-colored terrier was lying on the rocks below, with large waves washing back and forth across her limp body. The tide was coming in, slowly but surely, and soon, those rocks would be completely underwater.

If he didn't hurry, the little dog would be swept out to sea!

4

The seawall was too high in that spot for the dog to jump down without getting hurt himself, so he galloped along the wall to find an easier way to get to the injured terrier. He found a section where there was mostly sand and beach grass, with almost no rocks. Well, that was more like it! He hopped over the wall, and just as he'd hoped, the sand cushioned his landing. Then, he made his way across the rocks to where the terrier was lying.

He barked loudly, and the terrier whimpered, holding up her crooked right paw. She had escaped from her yard earlier this morning, and came down to the seawall to play. Unfortunately, she had slipped over the edge and fell awkwardly onto the jagged rocks. Her leg hurt so much that she couldn't walk and she had been lying there ever since, terrified that she would drown. Her wiry fur was soaked from the waves and her whole body was shaking uncontrollably from the cold.

She was very small, so the dog picked her up by the scruff of the neck as gently as possible. He carried her along the rocks, watching every step so that he wouldn't slip. If he dropped her by mistake, she might get hurt even more badly! Once he got to a place where the wall was low enough, he climbed onto a rock and set her down on the seawall. Then, he jumped up next to her, and moved her down to the sidewalk, out of the wind.

While the terrier was resting from her fright, the dog stood by the edge of the street and barked his most booming bark. A passing car stopped immediately, and the woman driving it got out to see what was wrong.

"Is everything okay, Santa Paws?" she asked curiously. Then, she saw the injured terrier. "Oh, no! Poor little thing. We'd better take her right to the vet."

The dog picked the terrier up and lifted her into the backseat as the woman opened the car door for him. Then he hopped in next to her, so that he could keep her company on the ride over.

Once they were at Dr. Kasanofsky's office, the dog carried the terrier inside and brought her to the front reception desk.

"Dr. K.!" his assistant shouted. "We need you. Santa Paws brought in another emergency!"

Dr. Kasanofsky came out right away.

"Good for you, Santa Paws," he said, and brought the terrier into a treatment room for X rays. She was a regular patient of his, and his assistant called her owners to come over right away. It turned out that the terrier, whose name was Tandy, had a broken leg, but that she would be okay once it healed. Her owners were very grateful that she was safe, and hugged Santa Paws several times.

While he was waiting for Tandy's cast to dry, Dr. Kasanofsky came out to thank Santa Paws and check the paw he had blistered the other day.

"It's much better, Santa Paws," he said, "but you really need a vacation. Doctor's orders!"

The dog barked and was delighted to accept several small biscuits from him. Running around so much had made him feel hungrier than ever. Dr. Kasanofsky was going to call Mr. Callahan to come and pick him up, but the nice woman who had driven him over with Tandy gave him a ride home, instead.

It was great to see his house again! The dog wagged his tail, barked a good-bye, and jumped out of the car. He ran straight up to the back door and scratched his paw across it.

Mr. Callahan opened the door, looking very relieved to see him. Dr. Kasanofsky had called to explain what had happened and say that Santa Paws was on his way home.

"Well, come on in, Pumpkin," he said. Mr. Callahan was the only person in the world who ever called him "Pumpkin," and the dog liked having a special nickname. "I'll fix you some lunch."

"Lunch" was a wonderful word. Almost as nice as "supper." The dog wagged his tail and went inside. After lunch, he might even get to take another nap!

Later that afternoon, Mr. Callahan went out, *all by himself.* It was a nightmare, and the dog flung himself onto the kitchen floor in despair. He moped as long as he could stay awake, which was about ten minutes. But he woke up the second he heard the back door opening. His family was home! Finally!

"Where's my buddy?" Gregory asked, and dropped his books, his gym bag, and Patricia's knapsack and hockey stick on the floor.

The dog barked, and leaped up to dance around with Gregory. He wasn't really allowed to jump on people, but Gregory was different. For one thing, he thought it was funny if he got knocked down by accident. So they had a regular ritual of doing a little dance together whenever Gregory came home.

"I'm fine, Mom. *Really*," Patricia was saying as she came in, although her right arm was in a sling.

The dog stopped dancing. Was Patricia hurt? Worried, he dropped to all fours and sniffed the sling delicately.

"It's okay, Santa Paws," she said, and patted him with her good hand. "I just separated my stupid shoulder. It's no big deal."

Mrs. Callahan, who was carrying her briefcase, along with the rest of Patricia's hockey gear, looked rather cross. "You really shouldn't have gone back into the game if you were hurt. What were you thinking?"

"Of *winning*," Patricia said.

Gregory laughed. "Of impressing what's-his-name, you mean."

"I was not," Patricia said, frowning at him. "And his name's Alex."

Gregory knew that perfectly well, but it was more of a goof to pretend that he kept forgetting. Alex and Patricia were supposed to be "just friends," but they had gone to the Winter Fling dance together a couple of weeks earlier, and he called her on the phone pretty often ever since then. Since Alex was a junior, and was therefore older than Patricia was, Mr. Callahan didn't approve of him at all. Considering that he also was both intelligent — and a smart aleck — Mrs. Callahan hadn't made up her mind yet.

"Do you want to go upstairs and lie down, and we'll bring you a tray?" Mrs. Callahan asked.

Patricia shook her head, but was very cautious

as she sat down at the table. "I'm honestly fine, Mom. I'll be back on the ice right after New Year's."

"You'll be back on the ice when Dr. Jennings *says* you can go back on the ice," Mrs. Callahan said.

Patricia started to shrug, and had to wince. One of the players on the other team had checked her hard enough to knock her down during the second period, and she landed with all of her weight on her right shoulder. After the game was over, she had had trouble changing out of her uniform, and the coaches — and her parents — made her go to the Emergency Room. At the time, Patricia had mainly been mad that *she* got called for the penalty, when it was the other player who slammed into her.

"It looks like it hurts," Gregory said sympathetically.

"Maybe a little," Patricia admitted — and then avoided her mother's gaze.

Just then, Mr. Callahan arrived home with take-out pizza, salads, and hot garlic bread for everyone.

The dog smelled pepperoni and sausage. And cheese! How exciting! He also smelled vegetables, which didn't excite him at all. Abigail was so overcome by the scents that she leapt onto the table — and landed right on top of one of the boxes. Evelyn kept her cool and remained in her usual spot on the counter.

Gregory opened the box to find part of the cheese now stuck to the top. "Nice going, Abby," he said, while he scraped it back onto the pizza.

Once everyone — including the animals — had finished supper, it only took a few minutes to clean up the kitchen. Then, Mrs. Callahan sat at the table to go through the latest stack of written invitations and fan mail for Santa Paws. On what they all called "Letter Nights," Gregory and Patricia generally helped answer the fan mail, while Mr. Callahan kept busy filing the originals away, in case they needed them for future reference.

There was so much fan mail coming in lately — sometimes more than a hundred cards and letters a week — that they had actually had to create some form letters on the computer to respond to them. But they all agreed that signing them with a paw-print was just too cute for their tastes. So, instead, whoever was answering each letter would scrawl the words "Love, Santa Paws" at the bottom. That was *still* a little bit too cute, but none of them had managed to come up with a better alternative yet.

The phone rang just as they were getting started, and Gregory answered it. Then he covered the receiver.

"It's a *boy*," he whispered loudly.

Patricia was not amused.

"Did he ask you for a date?" Gregory wanted to know, once she had hung up, ten minutes later.

"He asked me if my shoulder was okay," Patricia said. Then she blushed a little and sat back down at the table.

Gregory started to make a crack about Alex maybe dialing the wrong number by mistake and just being polite about it, but Mrs. Callahan pointed sternly at him, and he stopped in mid-sentence.

"Just wait until you start liking someone," Patricia said. "I'm going to take out a full-page ad in the *Oceanport Oracle*."

Gregory actually already liked a girl named Tracy — maybe, sort of, a little — but he knew better than to mention it anywhere near Patricia. If he ever asked her for a date, Patricia would probably never let him hear the end of it.

The telephone rang again, and this time, it was Patricia's best friend Rachel wanting to make sure that she was okay — and to see if Alex had called her. They talked for a while, and then Patricia returned to the table to help with the fan mail. It was extra-heavy this week, because of Christmas being so close.

Mrs. Callahan was separating the various invitations and solicitations into three piles: Nos, possible Yeses, and definite Yeses. The definite

Yes pile was very, very small. Patricia caught a glimpse of one of the letters she was dropping into the towering No pile, and reached for it with her good hand.

"You're turning down the Boston Baseball Writers' dinner?" she asked. "Why can't we go?"

Mrs. Callahan took the letter and placed it firmly back on the No pile. "Patricia, what on earth would Santa Paws do at the Boston Baseball Writers' dinner?"

"Introduce us to the Red Sox," Patricia said logically.

Gregory looked up from a stack of fan mail. "We could meet the Red Sox? No way. That would be so cool!"

"It would also be exploiting our dog," Mrs. Callahan said. "So, we're definitely not going."

"What if the Red Sox are all dying to meet *him*?" Patricia asked.

Mrs. Callahan looked at her for a minute, and then grinned. "Nice try. You almost had me there." Then, she dropped the letter back onto the No pile, and picked up the next invitation from the still-unopened stack.

"She wouldn't let us be guests of the Patriots that time, either," Gregory reminded Patricia, who nodded grimly.

"They wanted him to *perform tricks* at halftime," Mrs. Callahan said. "Santa Paws doesn't perform tricks. It's beneath him."

Hearing his name, the dog thumped his tail against the floor a couple of times, but didn't bother getting up.

"But still, Mom. It was the *Patriots*," Gregory said. He loved the Patriots, win or lose — but he had to admit, "win" was better.

"I'm sorry, we're just not going to take advantage of Santa Paws that way. It wouldn't be right." Mrs. Callahan glanced at an invitation from the Oceanport Folk Music Festival, and dropped it in the No pile. "At this rate, I'm sure we'll be hearing from the Celtics and the Bruins one of these days, too."

Considering that her mother was a physics teacher, Patricia decided to hit her where she lived. "What if MIT calls? Would you say no to *them*?" MIT was the world-famous Massachusetts Institute of Technology — and a university held in very high esteem by scientists and engineers.

"We *did* say no to them," her mother answered. "Last summer. They wanted to use Santa Paws in a probability study."

The dog was so sleepy that he didn't bother opening his eyes, but he thumped his tail again.

Gregory, however, was outraged. "They wanted to do experiments on him?"

"No, it was actually good science. They were proposing a very interesting — " Mrs. Callahan paused, and glanced over at Patricia. "But, luckily, I wasn't at all tempted, and we promptly turned them down."

"Good for us," Patricia said, with a little extra irony.

Mrs. Callahan grinned sheepishly, and busied herself with the invitations.

"You know, I think it would be a whole lot more fun if we just played Monopoly," Gregory said.

Mr. Callahan was on his way to the filing cabinet with another sheaf of letters, but that got his attention. "Monopoly? Oh, absolutely. That would be much better than this."

"Sounds great," Patricia agreed.

Mrs. Callahan pushed the stacks of invitations away and cleared a large space on the table, so that they could set up the game. "Works for me," she said.

The next day, the dog followed his usual pattern of eating, sleeping, chasing Abigail, and going outside to run around in the backyard every couple of hours. Nothing very exciting happened, except that he jumped over the fence once to help Jane, their mail-person, pick up some scattered letters. One other time, he dashed across the street to help Mrs. Lowell carry in some kindling, but that wasn't very eventful, either.

Then, after lunch, Mr. Callahan took out the

dog's toothbrush and grooming kit. The dog got very excited, because that meant he would be doing some visiting today. Where would they go? Who would they meet? Would the people give him treats? It was almost too exciting to imagine.

Abigail slunk off into the den as soon as she saw the toothbrush, and the dog knew that she would not be coming along this time. As far as he was concerned, she was very foolish. Why would anyone turn down a chance to go for *a ride in the car*? It just didn't make any sense to him.

Evelyn perched up on the kitchen counter to watch the tooth-brushing, which she found quite entertaining. She did not enjoy having *her* claws clipped, but she liked watching it be done to Santa Paws and Abigail.

Once he was all cleaned up, Santa Paws found his harness and bandana on the floor in Gregory's room and brought them to Mr. Callahan.

"Not yet, Santa Paws," Mr. Callahan told him. "We have to wait until the others get home. They're going to take you."

The dog knew the word "wait," and he didn't like it very much. It meant that whatever he was hoping to do wasn't going to happen for a while. So he paced around the house, lifted his paws onto windowsills to look outside, and barked every now and then. Naturally, he found some spare time for a couple of quick naps, but then he would return to pacing. Where were they? What was taking so long? Would they ever get here?

Finally, Gregory and Patricia and Mrs. Callahan came home. The dog bounced with joy, and barked quite a lot, too. In the car, Patricia had admitted that her shoulder really hurt, so she was going to spend the afternoon resting, instead of going back out. Mr. Callahan was working on his book, but he was also going to keep an eye on her, and maybe even bring her a tray or two of snacks.

Gregory changed into his official sweatshirt from the Oceanport Pet Therapy Team, because it was better to look somewhat official when they were visiting the hospital. People felt more at ease that way. Basketball practice had been suspended until after New Year's, so except for a half day of school the next day, it felt almost as though Christmas vacation had already started.

Mrs. Callahan sent him back upstairs to comb his hair, and then Gregory returned, picking up the bandana and harness from the kitchen table.

"You ready to go, boy?" he asked.

The dog barked so much that he almost ran out of breath, and he turned in circles a few times, for good measure. He was *definitely* ready to go.

In fact, he could hardly wait!

5

This particular afternoon, they were paying a visit to the pediatrics ward at Oceanport Memorial Hospital.

"It's awful that there are kids who have to spend Christmas in the hospital," Gregory said, as they drove over.

Mrs. Callahan nodded. She always found it difficult to visit the pediatrics ward, and it reminded her to feel very grateful for every moment that her own family was well, and safe. "I know. I hope seeing Santa Paws will help them feel a little better."

Inside the hospital, the dog knew exactly how to behave. He wore an extra-short leash, attached to his harness, and walked quietly next to Gregory's side. They stayed near the wall, so they wouldn't get in the way of any patients, visitors, or hospital workers. Even so, everyone who passed said hello, or at least waved. Santa

Paws was a familiar — and welcome — sight at the hospital.

The pediatrics ward was a large room, with brightly colored paint on the walls, and lots of beds. Sunshine streamed through the tall windows at the end of the room, and there were plenty of toys and games available. The nurses and orderlies were friendly and cheerful, and the children themselves were almost always full of smiles, too. Sometimes they were *brave* smiles, instead of happy smiles, but they were still smiles. A bunch of them shouted, "Hi, Santa Paws!" as soon as he came into the room. There were quite a few parents there, too, many of them looking tired and worried. But their faces relaxed a little when they saw Santa Paws prance in, wearing his jaunty bandana around his neck.

The dog started at one end of the room, and he took turns greeting every single child. He shook paws, he stood with his front legs resting on beds, and he kissed small faces whenever it seemed to be a good idea to do so. Since the children almost always liked having a souvenir from their special visit, Mrs. Callahan had brought along a Polaroid camera and plenty of film. She would take a picture of anyone who wanted to pose with Santa Paws, or one of Santa Paws by himself, if that's what they preferred. Then, they could keep it by their bedsides and look at it whenever they felt like seeing Santa Paws again.

One of the nurses found a rubber ball somewhere, and the children who were strong enough took turns throwing it across the room for Santa Paws to fetch. Sometimes he would bring it back to the wrong person — on purpose — and everyone would laugh.

When he came to children who didn't feel very well, the dog would just lean against their beds, or sometimes — if he was given permission — climb right up next to them for a few minutes. One little girl had been crying, because she felt sad, but Santa Paws had her giggling in no time by lying on his back on her bed and sticking his paws straight up in the air. A small boy had been too tired to eat his lunch earlier that afternoon, but now that he had a chance to share some of it with Santa Paws, he sat up and finished almost every bite!

Gregory had no idea how his dog knew exactly what each child wanted, without ever being given any instructions, but he had seen it happen so many times that he knew Santa Paws had a special instinct for all of this. And *his* instinct was always just to step aside, and let it happen.

Lots of the parents went up to Mrs. Callahan to thank her for making their children so happy. Naturally, she gave Santa Paws all of the credit, since she felt like nothing more than a witness.

Down by the windows, a little boy with a blond crewcut was sitting in a wheelchair. He was so exhilarated by the thought of actually meeting *Santa Paws*, that he was finding it hard to wait his turn. His legs hung limply in front of him, but he drummed impatiently on his wheelchair with his hands.

Finally, Santa Paws headed in his direction, and the boy's face lit up. His name was Jason, he was eight years old, and he had been in a very bad car accident back in November. So far, he was not recovering very well, and his parents were terribly worried about him.

On his way over, Santa Paws hesitated. Then he sat down about eight feet away from the boy.

"Come *on*, Santa Paws," Jason said, sounding completely frustrated. "Please come over here."

The dog wagged his tail, but stayed where he was.

Jason clapped his hands. "Come here, Santa Paws, Good dog!"

The dog kept wagging his tail, but still didn't move.

Jason was so discouraged by Santa Paws refusing to spend time with him that he almost burst into tears. "What's wrong with your dog?" he asked Gregory.

Gregory shrugged, since he had absolutely no idea. Santa Paws had never done anything like this before. "I don't know. Um, maybe he's tired, or — well — " He tried to give Santa Paws a subtle nudge with his foot, but the dog wouldn't budge.

"It's because he doesn't like me," Jason said, rubbing his eyes with one hand so he wouldn't cry. "Right?"

Gregory shook his head. "No way. He's just — I don't know. He's a *dog*. Maybe he needs to rest for a minute."

None of this made sense to him, and Gregory looked over at his mother for help.

Mrs. Callahan looked just as confused, since it was completely out of character for Santa Paws to disappoint a child.

"*Make* him go over there," Jason's mother muttered to Mrs. Callahan. "Can't you see how upset my son is getting?"

"I'm so sorry," Mrs. Callahan said, already on her way across the room. "This really isn't like him."

One of the nurses decided it was time to put a stop to this. She wanted the visit to cheer her patients up, not make them unhappy. "Maybe you should just take him home now," she suggested. "We can try a visit another day."

While they were all talking, no one had noticed that Jason was slowly, painstakingly, trying to stand. He used his arms to push himself up, and attempted to put weight on his legs. They were so weak and shaky that he almost fell down, and he clutched at the sides of the wheelchair for support.

The dog wagged his tail, and raised one paw invitingly.

"I *can't*," Jason said, crying a little. "Don't you see that I can't, Santa Paws?"

The dog just sat back on his haunches, and waited.

Jason took one tentative step, still afraid to let go of his wheelchair.

"This is just awful," Jason's mother was saying in a low voice. "The last thing he needs is a setback like this. The doctors have almost given up on his ever being able to — " Suddenly, she saw what was happening, and she gasped.

Realizing what was going on, the entire room was now silent. Everyone watched as Jason took one clumsy step, and then another. He took a third, and then a fourth, staggering his way over to Santa Paws. Then, he realized that he was walking — actually *walking* — and he stumbled the last few feet over to the dog and flung his arms around his neck.

"Look, Mom!" he yelled. "Look what I did!"

Almost everyone began clapping — and his mother wasn't the only one who had tears in her eyes.

"I walked to him!" Jason said triumphantly. "All by myself! Look at me!"

The dog let the little boy hug him, and then he

stood up very carefully. He could tell how exhausted the boy was from taking those first steps after so many long weeks of being crippled, and he led him back to his wheelchair, letting Jason hang onto his harness for extra support the entire way. He stood by protectively until Jason was sitting down again, and then he lifted his paw for him to shake.

Jason's mother rushed over to hug her son, and he told her over and over about how he had walked, that Santa Paws had fixed him, and when could he try walking again?

Santa Paws went to lean against Gregory's legs, and Gregory could feel that his dog was a little tired, too. He patted him on the head, but couldn't think of a single thing to say after what he had just seen.

"Good dog," he managed finally.

The dog wagged his tail, since that was his very favorite thing to hear.

Gregory dug around inside his jacket pocket until he found an extra biscuit. "Want a Milk-Bone, boy?"

The dog wagged his tail even harder. Maybe "good dog" was his *second* favorite thing to hear!

Driving home, it was quiet in the car. Santa Paws was sound asleep in the backseat. Even though he was full of pep *during* visits, afterward, he was usually worn out.

"That was, um, pretty okay," Gregory said at one point.

"It certainly was," Mrs. Callahan said, and they rode home the rest of the way in contented silence.

The first thing Gregory wanted to do — after feeding Santa Paws — was run right upstairs and tell Patricia the whole story about Jason. Unfortunately, one of the biggest rules of pet therapy was that it was considered unethical to tell anything personal about any of the patients he met — to *anyone*, even his own sister. Protecting the patients' privacy was extremely important. So, as much as he wanted to share the story, he knew that he couldn't.

But, he still went upstairs to her room to see how she was feeling.

Patricia was eating chips and salsa with her good hand, and talking to her best friend Rachel on her cellphone, using the special earpiece and headphone set.

"How's your arm?" he asked, after she finally hung up.

Patricia checked the door to make sure that no one else was listening. "It hurts a lot, but don't tell Mom and Dad. They might make me miss the rest of the *season*."

Gregory nodded. Patricia was probably going to try to play much sooner than she should, but at the same time, his parents were going to be overly cautious about letting her go back. With luck, it would work out somewhere in the middle. He helped himself to some of the chips and dug into the salsa, too.

"How'd it go at the hospital?" she asked.

"Good," Gregory said, and couldn't help grinning broadly. "Really, um, good."

When he didn't elaborate, she nodded. "Oh. Patient confidentiality," she said. She knew the rules as well as he did.

Gregory nodded. He and Patricia told each other almost everything, so he really didn't like to keep secrets from her. Especially a secret as exciting as this one.

"But something cool happened," Patricia guessed. It was easy to tell, since his expression was exactly like his "Hey, the Patriots just won the Super Bowl!" expression.

Gregory nodded. "*Very* cool."

Santa Paws was just the best dog ever.

Mrs. Callahan had been equally cautious about giving Mr. Callahan specific details, but he instantly understood that Santa Paws had done something more impressive than usual. He was happy to know that someone at the hospital had been helped by Santa Paws, even if he wasn't sure exactly how it had happened.

They all ate dinner up in Gregory and Patricia's parents' bedroom. That way, Patricia could rest on the bed with her arm propped up on some pillows, and at the same time, they could all watch a movie together. They had baked chicken with mushroom sauce, rice, acorn squash, and green beans.

Santa Paws napped on the floor near the fireplace, waking up whenever there was a possibility that someone — usually Gregory — might give him a piece of chicken. Once, Abigail intercepted the meat before he could grab it, and he was so disappointed that Mrs. Callahan gave him *two* small bites to make up for it.

The plan was for them to leave the next afternoon for Boston. They were going to stay for two days, and then drive back to Oceanport on Christmas night. Aunt Emily had already left early that morning, with her daughters Miranda and Lucy. Uncle Steve had to work, but he expected to join all of them in Boston sometime late on Christmas Eve.

Gregory and Patricia didn't know Aunt Emily's parents, the Harrisons, very well, so they felt a little shy about spending Christmas there. But, it *would* be fun to be in Boston, and see if holiday celebrations felt different in the city than they did in Oceanport.

After school let out at noon, they had a quick lunch of grilled cheese sandwiches and milk, before packing up the car. The cats were deeply suspicious about getting into their carriers, but once they saw the suitcases, they figured it was better than being left behind. Santa Paws was so ecstatic about the prospect of a trip, that he couldn't seem to stop barking.

Right before they left, Gregory took him for a walk around the block. He held tightly to the leash, because he didn't want to take any chance that Santa Paws might want to bolt off and rescue someone. He couldn't help feeling relieved when they made it back to the house without anything happening.

Finally, they were all sitting in the car, ready to go. Mr. Callahan checked to make sure that everyone was wearing seat belts, and then he started the engine.

They were on their way!

6

Boston was only about twenty-five miles away from Oceanport, but it seemed farther, because there was always so much traffic. After crawling along Route 128 for miles, they found an even bigger logjam on Interstate 93. The highway looked more like a parking lot than anything else, and according to the car radio, the traffic was that bad practically all the way to Quincy, a large town south of Boston.

"What if I got off in Medford, cut past Tufts, went through Harvard Square, and then took one of the bridges to Storrow Drive?" Mr. Callahan said to Mrs. Callahan.

Mrs. Callahan shook her head. "Too far out of the way. Go through Somerville to the Monsignor O'Brien, and then, we can go straight up to the Hill."

"Or we could chant a magical incantation, have the car morph into a hovercraft, and *fly* into town," Patricia said.

Gregory laughed, but their parents continued their conversation without missing a beat. Traffic jams made them both very tense, and inclined to bicker. At some point during all of this, it started snowing. The flakes looked very pretty, but the visibility was terrible, which slowed traffic down even more.

"We should have just taken 1A," Mr. Callahan said, tapping his fingers on the steering wheel. "It's so much easier."

"What, and deal with the airport?" Mrs. Callahan asked. "And the *tunnels*?"

In the end, they just stayed on the expressway until they got to the first Boston exit, and took it directly into the city.

Mr. and Mrs. Harrison owned a brownstone on Pinckney Street, near the very top of Beacon Hill. There was no such thing as an open parking space on Beacon Hill, so after helping unload the car, Mr. Callahan was going to move it down to the nearest garage.

Boston was a beautiful city, but Beacon Hill was special. It was very steep, with slim red brick rowhouses crowded next to one another, above uneven sidewalks also made of red brick. The quaint, cobblestoned streets were narrow, and lit by old-fashioned gas lamps instead of regular street lights. Small, well-tended trees added to the peaceful atmosphere. In the middle of a crowded city, Beacon Hill felt like a small, very exclusive town — and looked like it belonged on the front of a holiday card.

It was still snowing, with the flakes falling softly, but steadily. The dog was so excited about being in a new place that Gregory took him for a short walk to help him calm down before going inside. There were so many unfamiliar smells and sounds that the dog wanted to explore every different direction at once.

"What do you think, boy?" Gregory asked cheerfully. "You like being in Boston so far?" He was actually pretty happy to be in the city, too — it was so different from Oceanport!

The dog wagged his tail and barked once. Then he went back to sniffing lamp poles, mailboxes, trees, and everything else they passed.

Since it was dusk, the gas lamps were coming on, and the sidewalks were starting to get slippery from the snow. It had been perfectly clear when they left Oceanport, so Gregory was wearing his basketball sneakers instead of his hiking boots. That made it a little more difficult to keep his balance.

"Why don't we go back, boy," he said, "and you can have a treat."

A treat! Yes! The dog forgot all about the intriguing city smells when he thought about how nice it would be to eat a treat. And soon, he hoped, it would be suppertime! So far, this was a *wonderful* trip they were on.

They had taken a couple of turns, and Gregory stopped to get his bearings. They were standing somewhere near the top of the hill, and the streets were so steep that they seemed to go almost straight down with no slope at all. He was pretty sure that if they turned right, it would take them back to the Harrison's brownstone, although some of the little alleys and unexpected dead-ends were confusing.

The dog was ready to go left, but he happily followed Gregory the other way. Then, they heard a woman screaming.

"Help!" she shouted. "Oh, please, somebody help me!"

The dog ran away so quickly that he jerked the leash right out of Gregory's hands. Gregory chased after him, worried that his dog would get lost in the middle of the city. He called for him to come back, even though he knew that Santa Paws wouldn't pay attention. For his dog, rescues *always* came first.

He could see a woman running down the hill, slipping and sliding on the dusting of snow. She was obviously frantic, but Gregory couldn't see what was wrong.

Santa Paws loped gracefully past her, his stride confident and easy. Hearing the woman's cries, a couple of other people were also running down the hill, but the dog passed them with no effort. Gregory stopped long enough to rub some snow out of his eyes, so that he could see better, and then he realized what they were all chasing.

It was a baby carriage, rolling out of control, and heading directly for the busy street at the bottom of the hill!

At the last second, the dog lunged for the carriage and grabbed the handle between his teeth. He pulled back with all of his strength, but the carriage had picked up quite a bit of speed on its way downhill and it was hard to slow its momentum. The dog was having trouble getting any traction on the cobblestones, and the falling snow made it much more difficult. The carriage was dragging him downhill, no matter how hard he tried to stop it.

Gregory watched in horror as Santa Paws and the carriage skidded toward the rush-hour traffic on Cambridge Street. His dog — and the baby — were going to get hit by the cars!

Using all of his strength, the dog managed to slow the carriage down, and it finally stopped less than a foot from the cars speeding past them. Without letting go of the handle for even a second, the dog dragged it up to the safety of the sidewalk. Then he sat next to it, panting heavily.

A crowd of people gathered right away, with the baby's mother — and Gregory — close behind. Everyone was talking at once, and the mother was crying as she picked up her baby to make sure he was okay. The baby was only a few months old, and he seemed more confused than scared. He blinked a lot from inside his puffy plaid snowsuit, and then smiled when he realized that his mother was holding him. Apparently, she had slipped when she was crossing the street at the top of the hill, and lost her grip on the carriage. Watching it roll down the street had been like seeing one of her worst nightmares come to life!

Being surrounded by so many strangers made the dog feel edgy, and he was relieved when Gregory caught up to him.

"Good dog," he said, trying to get his breath. "You are a *very good* dog."

The dog wagged his tail and lifted one snow-covered paw so that Gregory would clean it for him. Gregory took off his gloves and bent down to clear the ice crystals away, and check his other paws while he was at it. If there was anything Santa Paws hated, it was getting ice stuck between his toes.

"I don't know how to thank you," the baby's mother said to Gregory. She had stopped crying, but she was still trembling. "How on earth did you get your dog to do that?"

Get him to do it? Gregory had to grin. He was pretty sure that there was no possible way to train someone — a dog *or* a person — to be a hero. And if there was, he wanted to learn how to do it himself. In his dog's case, it just came naturally.

"Wait a minute," a woman in the crowd said suddenly. "That's no dog — that's Santa Paws!"

The name "Santa Paws" caused a great flurry of excitement, and the size of the crowd seemed to double within seconds.

Gregory sighed. They had only been in Boston for about fifteen minutes, and his dog's cover was already blown. He wanted to deny everything, but his parents didn't like him to lie. Ever. It would probably be better if he just didn't say anything at all.

"Hey, that *is* Santa Paws," someone else in the crowd said. He happened to work for a local television news station, as a sound engineer, and he whipped out his cellphone to pass this information along to the news division right away. "Charlie, you need to get a crew over to Cambridge Street," he said into the phone. "Santa Paws is in town, and he just saved a baby." He listened briefly. "I don't know, let me check." He turned to Gregory. "Is he your dog? Are you living here now?"

The last thing his parents would want would be for him to broadcast the details of their holiday plans. "I'm sorry, I, uh, I really have to go," Gregory said. "Will you all please excuse us?" He smiled at the baby's mother. "I'm really glad your baby's okay."

People were still asking questions, and one woman was even taking pictures with a small camera she had been carrying in her purse. At first, Gregory was afraid some of them might follow him, but since it was the middle of a big city, he hoped that they had better things to do. Just in case, he took a fairly complicated route back to Pinckney Street — which was made even more complicated by the fact that he got lost at one point, and had to retrace his steps for several blocks to find his way.

He realized he must have been gone longer than he thought when he ran into his father already coming back from the parking garage.

Mr. Callahan looked surprised to see them. "I thought you two were just going around the block."

"Yeah, I know. Santa Paws rescued a baby," Gregory said, glumly. "It was about to get run over."

"Well — " Mr. Callahan frowned, not sure why his son looked so disappointed. "That's good, isn't it?"

"A bunch of people recognized him, and I think one of them was a reporter," Gregory said. "He was like, calling it in when we left."

Mr. Callahan winced. "Ooh. That didn't take long, did it?"

Gregory shook his head. In fact, less than

twenty minutes was probably a new record for Santa Paws.

"Well, let's hope it was a fluke," Mr. Callahan said. He was *determined* that the family was going to have a nice, normal Christmas this year.

Gregory nodded. Santa Paws had just been in the wrong place at the right time. Or maybe that was the right place at the *wrong* time. Anyway, what really mattered was that the baby was fine, and Santa Paws hadn't gotten hurt, either.

As they went into the brownstone, they were met at the door by a feisty little Shetland sheepdog. Her name was Becky, and she wasn't at all sure that she wanted some strange German shepherd to come into her house uninvited. It was bad enough that two *cats* had just arrived and impolitely made themselves at home. So she let out a series of fierce barks, and growled a little, too.

The dog backed away uneasily. He didn't spend very much time with other dogs, and he was never quite sure how to act around them. Mostly, he just wanted to wag his tail and be friends. But other dogs didn't always feel the same way, and sometimes they even wanted to start fights with him!

Mr. Harrison came out to the front hall to meet them. He was a retired judge, with white hair and a very deep voice.

"Sit, Becky," he said. "That's just Santa Paws. It's fine — he's a good dog."

The Shetland sheepdog responded with another flurry of high-pitched barks.

Santa Paws was a little unnerved, and he sat down. For some reason, small dogs alarmed him more than big dogs. Maybe it was because they were so little that he was afraid he might hurt them if he fought back.

Hearing all of the ruckus, Abigail marched downstairs from one of the guest rooms. She swatted Becky's right ear, and then gave Santa Paws a whack across the muzzle for good measure. All of that noisy barking had disturbed her nap.

Both dogs cringed, and Becky went over to sit next to Santa Paws, in case there was safety in numbers.

Pleased to have order — and silence — restored, Abigail stomped back upstairs. After such a long and grueling drive, she needed her rest.

Now Becky wagged her tail tentatively, and Santa Paws did the same to her in return.

"Good dogs, that's much better. Now, who would like to come into the kitchen and have a biscuit?" Mr. Harrison asked.

The dog's ears flew straight up when he heard that word. He wasn't quite sure who this man was, but he definitely liked him!

As the dogs followed Mr. Harrison to the kitchen, Gregory and his father found the rest of the family in the living room. There was a huge Christmas tree in the corner, with a genuinely astonishing number of presents piled underneath it. A fire was burning merrily away in the fireplace, and the mantelpiece above it was decorated with lights and holly leaves and garlands. The stereo system in the corner was playing a CD of Christmas carols, which added to the festive atmosphere.

Most of the furniture was solid old antiques, and from the way his niece Lucy was climbing around, it was obvious that the Harrisons weren't at all worried about things getting broken. That was good, because Lucy was only ten months old, and she was a true champion when it came to breaking things. Actually, since Gregory was pretty clumsy, he was fairly good at breaking things himself.

His cousin Miranda looked up from her crayons and drawing pad. "Hi, Gregory! Did you know that I am going to be *four years old* tomorrow?"

"I heard about that, yeah," Gregory said. He took off his Red Sox cap and put it on her head, which she always thought was funny, no matter how often he did it.

Miranda giggled, and stuck the hat on Lucy, instead. It was much too big for her, so it covered almost her entire face. She stopped crawling at once and sat down, baffled by why the room had suddenly gotten so dark.

Gregory put the hat back on his own head and looked around for a place to sit down. His mother and Aunt Emily were talking together on an overstuffed green velvet couch, and Patricia was sitting on a paisley love seat. Aunt Emily looked much more relaxed than usual, since most of the time, she was so busy, between commuting to work full-time here in the city and taking care of two toddlers.

Mrs. Harrison, who was plump in a reassuring, grandmotherly way, bustled over to give Gregory a mug of hot cider and some cookies. Mr. Callahan decided that he would rather have eggnog, and Mrs. Harrison pointed to the freshly chilled bowl on the buffet so that he could help himself.

"You were gone for quite a while, Gregory," she said. "I hope you didn't get lost. The streets around here can be a little confusing."

"Oh, no," Gregory assured her. "I mean, for a minute, maybe, yeah, but that was all. We just got — delayed."

Mrs. Callahan and Patricia looked up, since they immediately knew what he probably *wasn't* saying.

"Does that mean what I think it does?" Mrs. Callahan asked.

Gregory nodded.

"Did anyone recognize him?" Patricia wanted to know.

Gregory nodded, and everyone except for Miranda and Lucy exchanged glances.

"Well, it looks as though we're headed for another interesting Christmas," Aunt Emily said cheerfully.

So far, it didn't seem as though leaving Oceanport was going to make any difference at all. Apparently, Santa Paws was destined to be a hero *everywhere he went.*

7

The brownstone was bigger than Gregory and Patricia had imagined it would be. They had pictured a cramped city apartment, not a four-story house with spacious rooms and very high ceilings. The Callahans would be staying in the guest rooms on the top floor, with their parents taking one room and Gregory and Patricia sharing the other one.

Before supper, they went upstairs to unpack.

"Which one do you want?" Gregory asked, indicating the twin beds.

"The one by the windows, I guess," Patricia said. "You're not going to talk in your sleep or anything, are you?"

Gregory flushed. He had been told that he often had long conversations with himself while he was asleep. Obviously, he had never heard this for himself, so he wasn't completely sure if it was true. Whenever he asked Patricia to tell him what sort of stuff he said, her answer was always something along the lines of his talking, at length, about how much he admired her, and wished he could be more like her. Gregory figured that just meant that she was making the whole thing up.

"So, um, I guess they're kind of — rich?" Gregory asked, making sure to keep his voice low.

Patricia laughed, and looked around the room. "I'd say so, yeah."

Gregory thought about that briefly, and then shrugged. "Neat," he said.

Down in the living room, the dog suddenly began to feel terribly homesick. So he galloped upstairs to find Gregory and Patricia. They would make him feel better! He was running so fast that he almost crashed into the side of the doorway, and he bumped into a small mahogany chest in the hall. Several framed family photos displayed on the top fell over, and Gregory went out to put them back in the right places. Fortunately, none of them had gotten broken.

The dog whimpered anxiously, afraid that he had done something bad.

"Relax, boy," Gregory said. "Everything's okay."

The dog wagged his tail in response, followed him into the guest room and flopped down onto the braided rug between the two beds.

"Take a little nap, Santa Paws," Patricia said. "You'll feel better."

A nap. Yes! Patricia was so smart. The dog stood up, turned around three times, and flopped back down. Then he closed his eyes and was snoring softly within a minute or two. He slept soundly until he heard Mr. Callahan calling Gregory and Patricia downstairs for dinner. The dog had already been fed, but he followed them anyway, since he could smell ham, and he *loved* ham.

Mrs. Harrison and Aunt Emily had prepared a huge supper, with a baked ham, roasted yams, homemade rolls, steamed broccoli, and salad, with homemade apple pie for dessert. Mrs. Callahan had brought plenty of food from home — things like homemade brownies and loaves of bread, plus the special macaroni and cheese casserole that Miranda and Lucy loved. So some of that was on the table, too.

After dinner, except for Lucy and her grandparents, everyone walked down to Faneuil Hall and Quincy Market to look at the Christmas lights. Santa Paws and Becky came along, too. Back at the house, Lucy would be having her bath and going to bed. The Harrisons didn't mind babysitting, because as local residents, they had obviously been to Quincy Market countless times over the years.

On the way there, they passed the old African Meeting House building. Just to share a little history — Boston was *full* of history — Aunt Emily explained that during the fight against slavery in the 1800s, people known as abolitionists had gathered there regularly to give speeches and plan ways to eliminate slavery forever.

Patricia raised her good hand. "Excuse me. Will this be on the final?" She liked history, but hey, she was on *vacation*.

Everyone laughed, including Miranda — although she wasn't sure quite why. She just liked to feel included.

Considering that Boston was the site of the Boston Tea Party that helped trigger the Revolution, as well as Paul Revere's famous ride through the night to warn people about the British invading, and numerous other well-known events, there was a piece of history on almost every single corner. Gregory and Patricia had come to Boston on many school field trips over the years, visiting places as varied as the Museum of Science, the Museum of Fine Arts, a famous ship called the *USS Constitution*, and, of course, Fenway Park. They each had even walked the entire Freedom and Black Heritage Trails more than once.

Quincy Market was like an urban mall, except that it was more interesting than that. The complex was divided into three huge, long buildings.

Some of the shops inside were chain stores, but there were also lots of little pushcarts run by craftspeople, and other tiny businesses. Aunt Emily and Mrs. Callahan decided to take advantage of this by doing some last minute Christmas shopping for things like fancy candles, home-made earrings, hand-knitted scarves, and other small items.

The main building in the middle was a massive food court, with more different kinds of food than it would be possible to try out in a *month*. While Gregory and Patricia waited outside with the dogs, Mr. Callahan and Miranda went inside to buy fudge, and ice cream, and anything else that "looked interesting."

"Candy," Patricia said, after them. "Keep focusing on *candy*."

The entire marketplace, including the neat rows of trees, was decorated for the holidays, and there were streams of twinkling white lights everywhere. It was also very crowded, with throngs of tourists wandering all over the place. The snow was still falling, and there were already about three inches on the ground.

"Winter wonderland," Patricia said.

"Big time," Gregory agreed.

Becky was a city dog, so crowds didn't bother her at all. Santa Paws, on the other hand, spent most of his time sitting quietly between Gregory and Patricia, where he felt safer. However, there were so many wonderful smells coming from the food court that he pointed his nose in the air, and inhaled over and over. He could also smell the ocean, someplace nearby, and he found that very comforting, since it reminded him of home.

At eight-thirty, the whole family met in the open area in front of Faneuil Hall itself, which stood at the head of the marketplace. It was yet another historical landmark in Boston, where many famous speeches had been given over the years, dating all the way back to before the Revolutionary War.

On this particular evening, a choir was going to perform Christmas carols, followed by a group sing-along. Mr. Callahan had bought cups of hot chocolate for everyone, and the warm drinks tasted extra-delicious on such a cold, snowy night.

The music made the dog feel sleepy, and he took a short nap, leaning against Patricia's leg. He woke up when Becky yapped a couple of times, and then drifted off again.

Halfway through "Angels We Have Heard on High," there was a stir in the crowd behind them.

"Keisha?" a man's voice called softly. "Where are you, Keisha?" He shouldered his way politely through the dense crush of people, as he looked for his five-year-old daughter. The little girl had been standing right next to her parents and her brother, but now she seemed to have vanished into thin air.

The news filtered quickly through the crowd, and the choir paused long enough to ask if anyone had seen a small girl wandering around the area, wearing a green jacket and a striped stocking cap.

"I think that the girl was not holding her mommy's hand," Miranda said critically, as she clutched Aunt Emily's gloved fingers more tightly than she had been before. "Do you think so, too, Mommy?"

"It sounds that way," Aunt Emily agreed, looking concerned. "But *you* would never do that, right?"

"No," Miranda said. "Because I am going to be four, and four is too smart."

At first, it seemed like a routine incident of a child getting separated from her family in a large crowd. But as the minutes passed, and no one could locate Keisha, there was some noticeable hysteria in the air. The police had arrived and were fanning out in an organized search of the entire complex, but so far, they had had no luck at all.

Gregory looked at his parents. "Should we?" he asked. So far, no one had recognized Santa Paws, because his fur was quite snowy, and that helped disguise him. Being accompanied by another dog, Becky, also preserved the illusion that he was an ordinary German shepherd mix, out for an evening stroll.

"I'm afraid so," Mrs. Callahan said. "Come on." They made their way through the crowd to where the little girl's mother and brother were standing.

"Excuse me, I'm very sorry to bother you, but we'd like to help you find your little girl, if you'd let us," Mrs. Callahan said.

"Thank you," the little girl's mother, Mrs. Wyler, answered, sounding distracted as she scanned the crowd over and over, hoping to see Keisha. "She's wearing a red-and-white striped hat — it's her favorite."

Gregory cleared his throat. "Actually, we thought maybe our dog could help, ma'am. He's very good at finding things."

Mrs. Wyler nodded, so distressed that she barely glanced at them. "Yes, I'm sure he is. Thank you."

Her son Brandon tugged on her arm. "Mom, I think they mean it."

"I'm sure they do," his mother responded. She had been afraid to move from where they were standing, in case Keisha found her way back by herself — and then panicked when they weren't there anymore.

"Mom, it's *Santa Paws*," Brandon said. "Look!"

The name "Santa Paws" had its usual electric

effect, and people started coming over to confirm this sighting of the famous canine for themselves.

"Do you have anything of hers?" Mrs. Callahan asked. "He responds better when he has a strong scent to trace."

Mrs. Wyler held out a small blue mitten. "Here," she said, and almost burst into tears. "This is all anyone has found so far."

Gregory held the mitten close to the dog's nose. "You know the drill, boy. Find the little girl. *Fetch* her."

The dog knew those two words very well. He had located missing people, and objects, many times before. He sniffed the mitten, sniffed the air, and sniffed the mitten some more. Then he closed his eyes and lifted one paw so that he could concentrate.

There were so many people at this place, and so many smells! It was hard to pick out just *one*. But, if Gregory wanted him to do it, he would try as hard as he could. He circled around Brandon and his mother a couple of times, since the scent was very strong there. But then, it went off in two different directions! What was he supposed to do?

Puzzled by this, the dog sat down in the snow.

"Well, thank you for letting him try," Mrs. Wyler said, making an obvious effort to hide her disappointment. "I know he means well."

Gregory and Mrs. Callahan didn't worry about that, since they were accustomed to people doubting Santa Paws.

"You can do it, boy," Gregory said, and let him nuzzle the mitten again. *"Find* the girl, Santa Paws."

Santa Paws hated the idea of letting Gregory down, so he focused on the two different trails. Maybe he should just try one, and then try the other one. He got up and trotted toward the North Market Building.

Eager to see the great Santa Paws in action, a large group of people quickly swarmed after him.

"Hey, let's cool it!" Patricia said in her most authoritative voice. She had always wanted to be a police officer, although the United States Supreme Court and the world of vampire slaying also beckoned. "Give the dog some room to work!"

The starstruck group dropped back a little, but kept following him, whispering among themselves. The dog continued in a straight line and stopped right outside the entrance to a well-known local restaurant named Durgin-Park.

"I don't think that's going to help," Mrs. Wyler said unhappily. "That's just where we had dinner tonight."

Gregory shrugged. "Well, maybe she went back."

With Gregory's encouragement, the dog led him up the stairs and into the jam-packed restaurant.

"Hey, get out of here! No dogs allowed!" a cranky waitress shouted as soon as they walked in.

"No, wait, *celebrity* dogs are okay," one of the other waitresses said.

"Says *you*," the first waitress snapped, and then she slammed her way into the kitchen with an armload of plates.

The dog stopped next to a long wooden table, and looked up at Gregory for approval.

"Yes," Mrs. Wyler said. "That's where she was sitting."

The man who was currently sitting there was surprised to see that a large crowd had come into the restaurant to watch him eat, but he kept digging into his prime rib, anyway.

"Could I have a little bite of that, sir?" Gregory asked.

The man frowned at him, with his fork halfway to his mouth.

"It's not for me, sir," he said quickly. "It's for my dog. He needs a treat, and I don't have any."

The man shrugged, since he had no interest in some dog's troubles. "So what? Buy your own, kid."

The crowd was generally displeased by this response.

"For shame," someone said. "That's *Santa Paws*."

"You should give him a piece of meat," her companion agreed.

"It's un-American not to," a third person added.

The man had never enjoyed sharing, but he also didn't want to confront what might turn into an angry mob. Especially when he hadn't even been served his Indian pudding yet. So he cut off a chunk of the prime rib and gave it to Gregory, looking as disgruntled as possible the entire time.

"Thank you, sir," Gregory said, and gave the meat to Santa Paws. "You're a good boy. Now, find the girl!"

The dog swallowed the beef in one gulp, and instantly felt refreshed enough to resume his search. He led Gregory — and the growing crowd — out of Durgin-Park and back to where they had started. He knew that there was a second trail, but he couldn't quite remember where it was. So he methodically sniffed the snow until he picked up the scent again.

This time, he veered directly toward the food court.

"He's a big fake," a guy from Arlington muttered. "He just wants snacks."

"Yeah, really," his friend from Somerville agreed. "Like, total media creation. If we'd paid to watch this, I'm *wicked* sure I'd want my money back."

The dog stopped by the entrance and raised his nose in the air for a moment. No, the scent wasn't taking him inside — it was going along the side of the building, through the snow. So he followed the trail. Sometimes it went off in unexpected directions, and he had to dodge from side to side to keep on the right path.

"Showboat," the guy from Arlington said. "I bet he totally knows where she is, and he's just taking us for a ride, first."

A woman turned around to glare at him. "Will you two stop it? That's Santa Paws. Show some respect."

The two guys grumbled under their breaths, but decided to keep quiet for now. They wanted to stick around in case some television reporters showed up to cover the story. That way, they might get a chance to stand behind them during a live report and wave like crazy and shout "Hi, Mom!" over and over.

The dog didn't even notice how many people were behind him now, as he used every ounce of concentration to stay with the faint scent of the little girl. With the falling snow — and all of the people milling around — any tracks she had made were almost completely obscured, and the trail was fading, as a result.

He got to the corner of a crowded intersection,

and was stunned by the intensity of gas fumes, car exhaust, and rubber tires, as traffic drove by in both directions. He hated the odor of gasoline, because it always confused him. It also smelled *nasty*. On this corner, the car smells were so strong that he really couldn't hone in on anything else at all.

He had lost the scent!

8

When she saw Santa Paws slump down by the edge of the street, Mrs. Wyler began to cry in earnest.

"Someone please go get the police," she begged. "My poor little girl must have been kidnapped!"

It was a horrible thought, but if her trail stopped at a busy street corner, it was a definite possibility. Gregory looked at his mother to see if she had any advice.

"Let's try taking him across the street," Mrs. Callahan suggested. "The cars must be confusing for him." Although they had never done any formal training with Santa Paws, she had read a number of books about search and rescue dogs, and learned lots of different ways to assist them during searches, as a result.

When Mrs. Wyler saw them crossing State Street, she got even more upset. "Is Keisha all right? Did she get run over?"

On the other side of the street, the dog started sniffing again. It was snowing so hard now that a few flakes went up his nose, and he sneezed loudly. He looked surprised, and sneezed again, even harder.

"You okay, Santa Paws?" Gregory asked. Maybe all of the extra rescues he'd been performing lately were taking too much out of him. But, how could they stop now, with a little girl's life possibly at stake? "Here, maybe you need to smell this again."

He held out the mitten, and the dog buried his nose in the damp wool. Then he lifted his nose into the air one more time. Was there a tiny trace of — yes! There it was!

Confident that he had the trail now, the dog broke into a smooth trot. Gregory hung on to the end of the leash and did his best to keep up, because he didn't want to slow Santa Paws down and make him lose his concentration.

They ran up one block, down another, and then turned the corner. There, shivering in the small alcove of a commercial building, was Keisha! She was covered with snow, and her mitten-less left hand was exposed to the frigid air, but other than that, she looked fine. It was obvious that she was tired, but she wasn't crying. In fact, she appeared to be more perplexed, than frightened, by her misadventure.

The dog barked victoriously, and raced over

to her. He'd found the little girl! She was safe! Yay!

"Hi, doggie. I'm not allowed to talk to strangers," she informed him. "Or pat strange dogs. Because you might bite me."

The dog wagged his tail.

"Are you Keisha Wyler?" Gregory asked her.

The girl looked at him gravely. "You're a stranger. I'm not allowed to talk to you."

"Right," Gregory said, and took a couple of steps away from her. "That's a good idea. Make sure you remember that rule."

The little girl seemed to be okay, but she was obviously very cold, and he didn't think she would let him give her his coat and gloves to wear. It also seemed like a safe bet that she wouldn't allow him to take her hand and walk her back toward Quincy Market, either. And now that he thought about it, as far as that went, she probably *shouldn't*.

Where was the huge crowd of gawking onlookers when he needed them? He looked over his shoulder to see them heading in his direction, about a block away.

"Your mother's going to come here in a minute," Gregory said. "Do you mind if I wait with you?"

Keisha looked at him suspiciously. "If you stand — there." She indicated a mailbox about ten feet away.

"No problem," Gregory said, and went over to stand by the mailbox.

The dog thought that was unusual, but *lots* of things people did were unusual. Even the Callahans confused him sometimes.

"Keisha!" Mrs. Wyler yelled, when she recognized her daughter in the dim glow from the streetlights. "Keisha, are you all right?"

"This stranger is bothering me," Keisha said, pointing directly at Gregory. "He should go away now."

Gregory backed up, raising his hands in self-defense. "I was just, you know, standing here," he said to Mrs. Wyler — and his mother. "Honestly. She was very nervous about talking to me, so —"

"Relax, Greg," his mother said with a smile. "This is a happy ending."

Gregory realized that he had forgotten that part — and that he hadn't praised Santa Paws yet, either. So, he bent down to pat him and tell him how good he was, which pleased the dog very much.

"Maybe we should go buy him his own prime rib," he said to his mother.

Mrs. Callahan nodded. "Sounds like a plan," she said.

It took a little while to find Patricia and Mr. Callahan, who were busy looking for *them*. Aunt

Emily had already taken Miranda and Becky home, to get them inside for the night, and out of the snowstorm. Before they started heading back to Beacon Hill themselves, Mr. Callahan went up to Durgin-Park to get an order of prime rib to go.

A steady stream of people stopped by to shake paws with Santa Paws and congratulate him for being so clever. The Wylers had already left for the Emergency Room, where Keisha would have a check-up to make sure that she didn't have frostbite or any other signs of exposure. She had been out on her own in the snow — without her mitten! — for quite a long time. But the paramedics were confident that she was going to be just fine.

When they finally got home, the dog enjoyed every bite of his prime rib. Abigail, Evelyn, and Becky each had some, too. But the dog was very glad when it was time to go upstairs with Patricia and Gregory, and get ready for bed.

Before turning out the light, Patricia flipped on the television in their room so that they could watch the news for a while. It must have been a slow news day, because Santa Paws was the top story. The news station they had on had even created a special "A Hero Comes to Town" logo, and some original theme music to go along with it.

They had to laugh when they saw the guy

from Arlington and his friend being interviewed, standing in front of Faneuil Hall.

"We helped him a lot with the search," the guy from Somerville told the reporter, "but that dog is still wicked smart."

Gregory cracked up completely. "Do you hear that, Santa Paws? You even won over *those* two."

From his spot on the rug, the dog wagged his tail a couple of times. Then he yawned and let his eyes close.

It had been a very long day!

When they all got up the next morning, it was officially Christmas Eve and there were ten inches of snow on the ground. It seemed as though at least one reporter must have followed them back to Pinckney Street the night before, because by nine-thirty, the Harrisons had already gotten six phone calls from the press.

"I'm so sorry that you all have been inconvenienced like this," Mrs. Callahan said, as they all ate scrambled eggs, bacon, fruit salad, and toasted English muffins. "Maybe we should just head back home this afternoon, and let you have some peace and quiet."

"Oh, pish," Mrs. Harrison said, dismissing that idea entirely. She was a very jovial person, and a few pesky calls from reporters weren't nearly enough to get on her nerves. "It's a treat to have such a nice, crowded house for the holidays. Besides, he does good works. What's not to like about that?"

Mrs. Callahan was still concerned about whether their visit was creating too many problems, but Aunt Emily was quick to reassure her.

"Trust me, Mom is *not* shy about telling people what she really thinks," Aunt Emily said. "She wants you to stay."

Mrs. Harrison, who was scrambling another big batch of eggs, stopping stirring them for a minute. "There is one small thing, though."

Gregory glanced at Patricia, wondering if they were about to be sent upstairs to pack their bags.

"I'm on the board at the hospital," Mrs. Harrison explained, and gestured in the general direction of Cambridge Street. "They called this morning, and asked — well, since he happens to be in town, they thought — "

Gregory and Patricia were one step ahead of her. "Pet therapy," they said at the exact same time.

Mrs. Harrison nodded. "They'd love it, if he could stop by briefly today. I mean, unless you think it would be too stressful for him."

Everyone looked over at Santa Paws, who was lying on his back on the floor, playing with a tennis ball.

"Looks pretty tense to me," Patricia said.

With that, it was decided that they'd make

a Christmas Eve afternoon visit to the hospital. Gregory hadn't brought his harness or bandana on the trip, but Mrs. Harrison reminded him that she *was* on the board, and just this once, it would be okay to skip over a couple of the formal details.

After breakfast, Mr. Harrison put on his heavy wool coat and gloves, so that he could take Becky for a walk. Gregory and Patricia decided to join him, with Santa Paws. They also wanted to see what the city looked like, covered with a blanket of fresh snow. Patricia had to have her new Patriots jacket — she had finally grown out of her old one — zipped over her sling. She hadn't been complaining about pain at all, so Gregory figured that she was feeling okay. Either that, or she was just plotting the best, and fastest, way to get back on the ice.

Beacon Hill looked even more beautiful than it had the day before, with the trees covered with snow, and picturesque drifts all over the place. Mr. Callahan had gotten up early to shovel the sidewalk in front of the brownstone — and, to the delight of the Harrisons' next door neighbors on each side, he had gone ahead and shoveled their sections of sidewalk, too.

There were a few other people walking around, mostly with dogs, and they all seemed full of holiday spirit. Almost everyone they passed said hello to Mr. Harrison, so it was apparently a very close-knit neighborhood. Of course, it was also possible that they were all just *friendly*. Almost none of the streets up on the Hill had been plowed yet, but no one seemed to mind — and it wasn't exactly a good day for driving, anyway.

They walked down Joy Street toward Boston Common.

"Look at that," Mr. Harrison said, pointing toward the gold dome of the State House. "I've seen it thousands of times, but it's still wonderful."

Patricia and Gregory definitely agreed, but the dogs didn't seem to care at all. They were too busy jumping through drifts and barking at each other.

The Boston Common was a huge, sprawling park, which had originally been a cow pasture. Now it was just a nice place for people to enjoy, with walkways, benches, lots of trees, and playing fields. During the summer, city residents would often stretch out on the grass in their bathing suits to enjoy the sunshine, and the Common was the perfect place to enjoy a picnic lunch during the spring and fall.

Patricia's eyes lit up when she saw a large outdoor skating rink in the Common. "Hey, do you think Mom and Dad would let us go later?"

Gregory looked at her arm zipped inside her jacket. "*No*. I don't."

Patricia looked disappointed, but she didn't push it.

After walking through the Common, they crossed over to the Public Garden. During most of the year, the Public Garden was filled with brightly colored flowers and its lawns were always perfectly trimmed. It was much more elegant and formal than Boston Common. The center of the Public Garden was dominated by a large, man-made pond. During warmer weather, people would take leisurely rides around the pond in old-fashioned swan boats. Gregory and Patricia's parents had brought them here many times, when they were younger.

"It's a little bit of a walk, but would you like to go up and look at the Christmas tree at the Prudential Center?" Mr. Harrison asked.

Patricia and Gregory really liked walking in the snow — except for that Christmas when they had been lost in the middle of the White Mountains — so, they thought that was a great idea. The dogs were clearly enjoying this excursion, too.

Quite a few people recognized Santa Paws as they wandered along, and each time, they would come over to meet him, and maybe shake his paw. Some of them asked permission to take pictures, too.

"Is it always like this when you're out in public with him?" Mr. Harrison asked.

Gregory and Patricia both nodded. It always had been — and apparently, it always would be.

They were on Newbury Street now, and it was fun to look at all of the fancy stores with their windows lavishly decorated for the holidays.

Patricia shook her head, fairly amazed by the endless stream of exclusive shops. "I don't think I could afford a single thing on this entire street."

"Sure you could," Gregory said. "I bet there's a place around here somewhere that sells newspapers."

"That's true," Patricia conceded. "I could spring for that." Her parents didn't want her doing anything more demanding than some occasional babysitting during the school year, but they had promised that she could get an actual *job* during the summer, if she wanted. All of which reminded her that she wanted to ask Mr. Harrison what it had been like to be a criminal court judge for so many years.

Mr. Harrison had only been retired for about six months, so he still really missed being at the courthouse every day. As a result, he was happy to share stories about some of his more interesting cases, and judicial dilemmas.

"That's why I'm going to be a veterinarian," Gregory said, after hearing a few of the stories. "It's nice and simple. Animals get sick or hurt; you try to help them. I think I'd be pretty ner-

vous, having to be in the same room with crimi-
nals and all."

Mr. Harrison laughed. "Oh, it's not so bad. After a while, you get used to — "

Just as he spoke, they saw two people strug-
gling with each other about a block ahead of
them. One of them was a seedy-looking young
man in a beat-up black jacket, and the other
was an elderly woman with a cane. The man
wrenched something away from her, shoved her
into the nearest snow-drift, and took off.

"Stop!" the woman cried out. "Stop, thief!"

Witnessing this scene, the dog strained forward against his leash, visibly agitated, and
whining softly.

Gregory and Patricia looked at each other.
Then Gregory sighed and bent down to unhook
the leash from his collar.

"Okay, Santa Paws," he said, as he straight-
ened back up. "Go get him!"

9

Santa Paws charged up the street after the mugger. Even though the man had gotten a head start, the dog was much faster. Without even letting out a warning bark, he launched himself into the air and knocked the man down onto the snowy sidewalk. The man landed hard, and let his breath out with a grunt. He tried to get up, but Santa Paws stood above him, growling softly.

The thief raised one hand, and the dog's growl intensified.

"Okay, okay, take it easy already," the man said, so frightened that his voice practically squeaked. He was terrified of dogs — especially *big* dogs.

Then, to make matters worse, *another* dog appeared. This one was smaller, but it was barking like crazy.

The man ducked down, trying to protect his

face with his arms, in case they started attacking him.

Gregory, Patricia, Mr. Harrison, and the elderly robbery victim showed up next — arriving in that order.

"Well, he really *is* quite impressive, isn't he," Mr. Harrison said to Gregory and Patricia. He patted Santa Paws, and then turned his attention to Becky. She had tugged her leash away from him during all of the ruckus and gone charging fearlessly after Santa Paws. "And aren't *you* a good dog."

The elderly woman snatched her purse back from the mugger and checked to make sure that everything was still safely tucked inside.

"Well, I never," she said huffily. Her name was Elsa Talbot, and never, in all of her years, had anyone dared to *shove* her like that, to say nothing of robbing her. "We'd better call the police, right away."

That seemed like a good idea, and all four of them pulled out their cellphones and then stared at one another.

"Do we *all* call?" Gregory asked.

"You can do it, Greg," Mr. Harrison said. "Unless," he tipped his hat respectfully in the elderly woman's direction, "you'd prefer to do it yourself, ma'am."

Mrs. Talbot shook her head. "No, let one of

these nice children call. I want to keep my eye on our prisoner." She hefted her cane. "If he tries to run again, I'm going to *whomp* him one."

So Gregory called 911, and they waited for the police to arrive. After the whole family had gotten separated during an ice storm the previous Christmas, their parents had decided that it would be a good idea if they all had cellphones. Gregory and Patricia had had to promise that they would carry them everywhere they went — and not waste too many of their monthly minutes talking to their friends. So far, they had been good about following the first rule, but not so great about the second one.

A police car pulled up a few minutes later, and two officers got out. They were very surprised to see the thief already captured, and lying in the snow with his hands clasped behind his head. That made him unusually easy to search and handcuff, especially since he was eager to do anything that would get him away from the dogs.

One of the officers came over to take a report, while her partner read the mugger his rights and ushered him over to the police car to be transported back to the station house. Mrs. Talbot spoke — at length — without letting anyone else get in a single word. She explained the nature of the errand she had been on, the fact that never, ever, not even once, in all of her days, had she been so rudely accosted, and then expressed her extreme desire to press charges and have the criminal repay his debt to society, preferably for a period of many years.

When she finally paused to take a breath, the police officer cut in.

"Okay, I think I have a pretty clear picture for now. We can straighten everything out down at the station," she said. Her name was Officer Ramirez, and her partner was Officer Peters. "Is the whole family going to come along with you?"

"Why, I've never seen them before in my life," Mrs. Talbot said, looking them over critically to make sure that was true. She wanted all of her statements to the police to be accurate in every way. "They're ordinary bystanders. Passersby. Good Samaritans, actually. In fact, I think —" She stopped to look at the dogs more closely. "My goodness, is that who I think it is?"

"Do you think it's Santa Paws?" Patricia asked, in case Mrs. Talbot had a notion that it was some other, well-known dog.

Mrs. Talbot nodded.

"Well, then, yes, it's who you think it is," Patricia said.

"My stars, I never would have imagined such a thing, in all of the world," Mrs. Talbot gasped. "Never, in my whole life. I've been rescued by Santa Paws! Me! Elsa Talbot! I'm going to have to go on television and tell my story. Yes, that's what I'll do. This very day. Sure, it's anecdotal

— but valuable, from an archival perspective? You *betcha*."

When Mrs. Talbot finally went off with the police to go swear out an official complaint, still chattering away without ever seeming to pause, Gregory, Patricia, and Mr. Harrison all let out their breaths.

"That was — " Gregory couldn't think of the right word, so he just shook his head.

"It sure was," Patricia agreed.

The mammoth Christmas tree at the Prudential Center was an awesome sight — in every sense of the word. They stood and looked at it for a while, as last-minute shoppers rushed past them, trying to complete their holiday shopping before it was too late.

When Santa Paws and Becky started fidgeting, they headed back toward Beacon Hill. Even during the short time they had been outside, the snow-plows had made some progress on the streets, and more sidewalks were being shoveled. So, the walking was much easier than it had been before. They were all a little bit tired, so it was just as well.

They were exiting the Public Garden, when they heard a splash — and a shriek. Santa Paws halted at once.

Patricia sighed. "You know, maybe we should

stop letting him go outside at *all*," she said to Gregory. "We could train him to use a litter box, or something."

He nodded, and then — with a look of resignation — unhooked the clasp on Santa Paws's leash again.

The dog tore back into the Public Garden, heading for the pond. A group of teen-aged boys had been fooling around on the big stone bridge above the water. They were throwing one boy's hat back and forth, and when he tried to grab it, he fell over the side of the bridge by accident.

The pond *looked* frozen, but it wasn't. The boy, whose name was Rick, crashed right through the inch or two of ice and into the frigid water beneath it. He didn't know how to swim, so he was utterly terrified.

One of his friends was getting ready to go in after him — even though he wasn't a very good swimmer, either — when Santa Paws appeared. The dog ran across the snow-covered pond, as the ice creaked and cracked underneath his racing paws.

Patricia was already calling 911, because she wasn't sure if Santa Paws was big enough to save the boy by himself. She and Gregory stood at the edge of the pond with Mr. Harrison and Becky, watching anxiously. Becky barked at the top of her lungs, running back and forth. She was afraid of the water, but she didn't want to see Santa Paws have to do all the work by himself, either.

"I should go in after him," Gregory said, already unzipping his jacket.

"You will do *no such thing*," Mr. Harrison said in such a firm voice that Gregory zipped his jacket right back up again.

Just then, the ice around Santa Paws caved in completely, and he disappeared beneath the water!

Gregory ripped his jacket off. "No way I'm letting my dog drown," he said, and then bent to untie his hiking boots.

Patricia was frustrated because she knew that there wasn't much she could do to help with her arm stuck in a sling. She looked around for something — *anything* — that they could use to rescue Santa Paws and the drowning boy.

There were lots of people walking their dogs in the Public Garden, and many of them had gathered at the shoreline, watching the drama with horror.

Santa Paws suddenly surfaced, dog-paddling energetically and spitting out water. Then he swam decisively toward Rick, using his paws to break through any shards of ice that were in his way.

The onlookers clapped and cheered, as they tried to encourage Santa Paws in his desperate attempt to save the boy. Rick had already gone under for the third time, and so far, he hadn't come back up again.

Patricia grabbed Gregory's arm just as he was about to leap into the pond, dressed only in his jeans, socks, and a turtleneck. "Leashes!" she said.

He stared at her as though she had gone completely crazy. "What?"

"There are dogs all over the park," she said. "Let's get all the leashes, connect them, and then we'll have a rope."

It was such a goofy idea that Gregory realized it might actually work. He cupped his hands around his mouth so that he could amplify his voice.

"Hey!" he bellowed across the pond. "We need your leashes to make a rope! Get the leashes over here, quick!"

Patricia was already snapping Santa Paws's leash to Becky's, which gave her a sturdy, makeshift rope about eight feet long. Dog owners came running over from every section of the Public Garden, holding out their dogs' leashes.

Thankful to have something to *do*, Rick's friends helped gather even more leashes, and brought them over to where Patricia was standing. Working together, using the metal clasps, or creating tight loops by threading the leashes through their own handles, they formed an increasingly long rope.

Out in the pond, Santa Paws kept diving underwater until he located Rick. He managed to snag the boy's jacket with his teeth, and dragged him slowly to the surface. Rick coughed and choked — and went right back under.

Gregory couldn't watch this for another second without pitching in somehow. "Sorry, Mr. Harrison, gotta go," he said, and abruptly dove into the water, aiming for a spot where the ice had already shattered.

He was actually an excellent swimmer, but the temperature of the water came as a complete shock to his system. It was so cold that he couldn't catch his breath, and he had to tread water to get his bearings. That made him feel even more cold, since moving around consumed so much body heat. But he headed for Santa Paws with a strong breast stroke, pumping his arms and legs extra-hard to try and swim faster.

Santa Paws had hauled Rick's limp body up yet again, but the boy was about sixteen and very heavy — with his water-logged clothes only adding to his weight. Rick's nose was just barely out of the water, but he didn't seem to be breathing anymore.

There was the sound of sirens somewhere in the distance, but it didn't seem as though they would be able to get there in time, because they were so far away.

Gregory swam over to Santa Paws.

"Hey, boy," he said, so cold that he had trouble remembering how to form words.

Santa Paws was startled enough to let go of Rick's jacket by mistake, and the boy sank below the surface again.

"It's okay, buddy," Gregory said, with his teeth chattering furiously. "We can do it."

The dog was very disturbed that Gregory was out here in the water, where it wasn't safe, but he forced himself to go after Rick one more time.

By now, the makeshift leash-rope was about eighty feet long, which would be more than enough.

"Okay," Patricia said. "Who has a good arm?"

One of Rick's friends stepped forward. "I do," he said, since he was a pitcher on his high school baseball team. He picked up one end of the rope and hurled it out into the middle of the pond as hard as he could. In fact, he threw so accurately that one of the leashes hit Gregory in the back of the head.

"Hey!" Gregory protested. The icy temperature of the water was already having a terrible effect on him, and his first jumbled thought was that someone was throwing snowballs at him, on top of everything else.

111

"It's a rope, Greg!" Patricia yelled. "Grab the end of the rope!"

Gregory couldn't quite make sense of that, but she kept yelling and pointing until he saw part of the leash-rope caught on a piece of unbroken ice. He picked it up with numb hands, and tried to find the end.

Santa Paws had hauled Rick back to the surface and was swimming toward Gregory, with Rick floating lifelessly along behind him.

Gregory knew he was supposed to do something with the rope, but he was having trouble remembering what it was. There seemed to be a lot of people shouting, but Gregory was able to pick out his sister's voice from the rest of the noise. After all, he was *used* to her telling him what to do.

"Tie it around him!" Patricia said. Part of her just wanted to pull her little brother in, and leave Rick to fend for himself — but she knew that she couldn't let herself think that way. Even though it was very tempting. "You can do it, Greg!"

Gregory's hands didn't want to work right, but he managed to wrap the rope around Rick's chest. Then he secured it with a very clumsy square knot.

At least twenty people were standing at the other end of the leash-rope, and working together, they tugged Rick through the water and ice, toward the shore. They pulled him up out of the water, and a woman who happened to be a nurse immediately began doing artificial respiration on him.

Gregory was very tired. It was cold. Very cold. He could still kick his legs, but his arms weren't working right anymore. More than anything, he really just felt like sleeping.

All he needed to do was sleep, for a minute, maybe, and then he'd be okay again. He closed his eyes, and felt himself slowly starting to slip underneath the water.

"Gregory!" Patricia shouted. "Gregory, don't! *Please.*"

Santa Paws was also losing strength, because of being in the frigid water for so long, but he kept his focus by concentrating on rescuing Gregory. He *loved* Gregory, and he had to keep him safe.

Rick's baseball-playing friend threw the leash-rope back out into the water, but Gregory didn't even notice. He was too busy just trying to stay conscious, and afloat.

But the dog saw the rope and he caught it between his teeth. He swam around Gregory once, and then again, so that the rope would loop around his body. Then, using every last bit of his remaining energy, he began swimming toward the edge of the pond.

"All right, pull!" Mr. Harrison said in his most

commanding voice. "Everybody, pull right now!"

With so many people working together, they were able to haul Gregory and Santa Paws over to the shore. Once they were almost within reach, Mr. Harrison and two other men waded out a few feet in the water to help guide them in the rest of the way.

Everybody else watching just prayed that it wasn't too late!

10

The air was loud with the sound of sirens, as the police, fire department, and ambulances finally began to arrive. They parked their vehicles along the boundaries of the Public Garden and ran to see how they could help.

Rick was breathing on his own again, but he was only half-conscious and needed to be taken to the Emergency Room right away. Paramedics had him bundled onto a gurney, and then inside one of the ambulances within a couple of minutes.

In the meantime, Gregory was conscious, but not making very much sense. Patricia had pulled his hat back onto his head, and put his jacket, as well as hers, on him. Santa Paws was so cold that his fur was actually covered with bits of ice, and he had been draped with Mr. Harrison's coat to try and help him get warm.

Since the crisis in the water was over, the police officers and firefighters didn't have much to do. The most pressing problem — other than getting Gregory and Santa Paws to the hospital as soon as possible — was crowd control. People were flocking into the Public Garden from all over the place, as word of the near-tragedy — and Santa Paws and Gregory's heroic efforts — quickly got out.

"It's hot," Gregory said, and tried to make his hands work well enough to tear off the two jackets he was wearing. "I'm really hot. Why do I have to wear these stupid things? Get 'em off me already."

Patricia was alarmed by that, but since the EMTs worked in a city accustomed to harsh winters, they had treated cases of hypothermia many times before and knew just what to do. They quickly put special oxygen units on Gregory and Santa Paws, which produced very warm, moist air. This would help bring their body temperatures back up to normal. They had also pre-warmed IV solutions on the way over, and had both of them hooked up before they were even hustled over to their ambulances.

Gregory kept trying to take his oxygen mask off, to get off the gurney completely, and to walk back to the house — in *Oceanport*. He couldn't sit still, and he had petulant complaints about absolutely everything that was going on. So the EMTs agreed to let Patricia accompany them on

116

the ride over, since she might be able to keep him calm.

In the meantime, Mr. Harrison had called ahead to the house, so that their parents would be able to meet them at the hospital. He was going to be driven home in one of the police cars, first, so that he could drop Becky off. Then he was going to come straight to the hospital, since he wanted to do anything he could to help.

Inside the ambulance, Gregory was very upset — and short-tempered, even though he couldn't quite explain why he was so angry. He immediately tried to yank out his IV, and then he tried to get off the gurney again.

"Where's my dog?" he kept mumbling. "I want my dog. Get me out of here. This is *stupid*."

Patricia picked up his hand. It was scary to see her little brother acting like this. He just wasn't a person who got agitated — even when it might actually be a good idea to do so. "Greg, he's fine. He's right behind us. Everything's okay."

"Take it easy, son," one of the EMTs, whose name was Andy, said, calmly replacing his oxygen mask again.

Gregory pulled it off and tried to throw it aside. "I'm not your son," he said, sounding as though his tongue was stumbling over the words. "My dad, *he* can say that. But, you? No way, man. Back off."

117

"Tough kid, hunh?" Andy said to Patricia.

Patricia shook her head, feeling as though she might start crying. "This isn't the way he is at all. He's like, the most friendly, easy-going person in the world. He never gets mad at *anyone*." What was wrong with him? Could being in freezing water have hurt his brain, somehow?

"Don't worry," Andy told her kindly. "It's one of the symptoms of hypothermia. He'll snap out of it as he warms up."

Gregory was muttering something about it's not being fair that he wasn't going to the Boston Baseball Writers' dinner — and then, he started moving around again and asking for Santa Paws.

Since she didn't know what else to do, Patricia just kept taking his hand. He'd shake free and tell her she was bugging him — and five seconds later, he'd be asking where his sister was, how come she wasn't keeping him company, and if she was okay. So, Patricia would pick up his hand again and keep talking to him, saying what she hoped were calming, soothing things. But she *really wished* that their parents were there with them.

When they got to the Emergency Room, the paramedics moved quickly. They rolled the gurney inside and straight to a treatment room. Patricia tried to follow them, but a nurse ushered her away. She tried again, and an orderly stopped her this time.

Patricia had never been inside a big city Emergency Room before, and it was even more crowded and noisy than she would have expected. Because of the heavy snow, there had been many more traffic accidents than usual, and there were patients with all sorts of other problems like food poisoning and the flu. It made her wonder if she would ever be able to watch a medical show on television again. Suddenly, that concept just didn't seem very entertaining, after seeing the real thing.

Patricia couldn't stand waiting for her parents to arrive, so she decided to call them herself, just to make sure that they were on their way. As she took out her cell phone, a security guard reminded her that she couldn't use it inside the hospital. So, she stood there, frowning, and wondering if she should try to find a pay phone.

"Why don't you step outside for a minute, miss, and you can call from there," the guard said kindly.

She was just leaving the ER to make her call, when her parents and the Harrisons rushed in. Patricia wanted to cry when she saw them, but she was afraid that that would make them worry too much, so she simply nodded and told them how glad she was to see them.

"Where are they?" her mother asked.

Patricia pointed toward the treatment rooms. "Back there. They told me I had to wait out here."

"Well, let's see about *that*," her mother said, and strode across the ER, with Mr. Callahan right behind her.

Her parents must have done a far better job of talking their way into the treatment room than *she* had, because they were immediately permitted to go inside. Mr. Callahan came out a few minutes later, looking somewhat calmer.

"He's going to be okay," Mr. Callahan said. "He's already responding." He ran one hand back through his hair, leaving a mass of cowlicks behind. "Which room did they put Santa Paws in?"

Patricia looked around, realizing that she hadn't seen him since they had come in. "I'm not sure. He was in a different ambulance."

"Well, let me go find out, then," Mr. Callahan said, and walked toward the main receiving desk.

"Do you think he knows that he's still wearing his slippers?" Mr. Harrison asked, watching him walk away.

Patricia smiled a little. "I doubt it." He'd never noticed before — why would today be any different?

When Mr. Callahan returned, he looked worried again.

"What?" Patricia asked, already dreading the answer.

"Santa Paws isn't here," Mr. Callahan said. "They don't know where he is."

Patricia could tell from the expression in his eyes that he felt like panicking almost as much as she did. They were all still haunted by the terrible Christmas when Santa Paws had been stolen, and — what if it had happened again? Or maybe the ambulance had gotten into an accident, or — she saw Andy, the EMT, just leaving the Treatment Area, and moved to intercept him.

"Hey, there," Andy said brightly, when he recognized her. "Looks like your brother is already bouncing right back." He winked at her. "Must be a tough kid, after all."

Patricia nodded. "Thank you. That's what my father just told me, too. But we can't seem to find our dog. Do you know which treatment room he's in?"

"Oh, they didn't bring him *here*," Andy said. "They diverted him over to Angell Memorial."

Patricia was going to say something to the effect of "*What?!*" but then she saw her father and the Harrisons nod. It turned out that Angell Memorial was a famous veterinary hospital in Boston — and the most logical place for Santa Paws to have gone.

"They're just wonderful over there," Mrs. Harrison assured her. "You can count on them taking excellent care of him."

That made Patricia feel better, but she still wished that they had brought him to this hospital, instead.

He was a hero, and he *belonged* here, with his family.

As he rode in the ambulance, Santa Paws began to feel better. He was still shivering, but not nearly as much as he had been a few minutes earlier. That water was so cold! It actually *hurt* to swim through it. Yuck! He hadn't liked it at all.

The warm saline solution and oxygen were helping his temperature get back to normal, and the blankets covering him were nice, too. But he missed Gregory and Patricia, so he whimpered a little. Where were they? Were they okay? Why had they let people he didn't even know take him away like this?

"Good dog," Victor, one of the EMTs, said to him, patting his head. "Don't be scared, Santa Paws."

The dog looked at him uneasily. Why did this man know his name? And where were they going? Something was wrong here, the dog just *knew* it.

"He must be the dog of steel," one of the other two EMTs, Mabel, said, as she did another in a series of checks on his vital signs. "His heart rate and respiration are completely normal. They may not even have to admit him."

"Do you hear that, Santa Paws?" Victor asked.

"Sounds like you just might be home for Christmas."

The dog stiffened. Were they taking him to his home — or to *their* home? What if they were bad people? He sensed that they were nice, but how could they be, if they were taking him away from Gregory and Patricia like this? What if they were going someplace very far? How would he *ever* get home? This was just awful.

"His pulse is going up a little," Mabel observed, as she double-checked his vital signs. "See if you can calm him down."

"Maybe he's worried about the kids," Victor said. "I mean, he risked his life trying to save them."

That made sense, and Mabel nodded. "I wish we could explain it to him. After everything he's been through today, it's not good for him to get so upset."

The dog allowed them to pat him, but he watched them suspiciously. These people might *think* they could take him somewhere he didn't want to go, like the bad robbers had that time, but they were wrong.

He would *never* let that happen again.

No matter what.

Back at the hospital, Patricia sat in the waiting room with the Harrisons. Her parents came out every so often, to say hello — and update her — but mostly, she just sat quietly, with her hands folded in her lap. Gregory was doing much better, and her mother promised that she would be able to go in and see him soon. Rick, the boy who had almost drowned, was also improving. He was conscious now, and able to speak, but he would probably have to spend a few days in the hospital to recover from his ordeal.

News of the dramatic water rescues must have spread fast, because the press had already begun arriving. Fortunately, the hospital security staff had requested that they wait outside instead of cluttering up the waiting room.

Earlier, Andy had been able to patch through to the ambulance taking Santa Paws to the veterinary hospital, and gotten a report back that his vital signs were excellent, and that they were still "en route." Since then, Patricia hadn't heard anything else, but he must have been admitted by now. She still didn't understand why they hadn't told her they were taking him someplace else, but — it was too late now, unfortunately.

She had no idea how much time had passed when her mother finally came out to bring her into the treatment room.

"Is he — acting like Gregory?" Patricia asked.

Her mother looked confused. "What do you mean?"

That meant that he was behaving like Gregory again. Patricia smiled for the first time since he and Santa Paws had jumped into the water in the first place.

In the treatment room, Gregory was lying in bed, covered with several thick layers of blankets and still connected to an IV. His face was pale, but otherwise, he looked just the way he always did, except for the fact that he was still noticeably shivering.

"How's Santa Paws?" he asked instantly.

Patricia wasn't sure if her parents had told him that he was over at the veterinary hospital, so she decided not to mention that particular detail. "He's fine. They said his vital signs are really good now."

Gregory looked very relieved. "When can I see him?"

Patricia glanced at her parents, since she wasn't quite sure how to answer that. "I haven't actually seen him yet, either," she said. "But I know he's okay. Are *you* okay?"

Gregory nodded, pulling the blankets closer. "Just, you know, um, tired and stuff. How's that guy we went in after? Is he doing okay?"

"I just spoke to his mother out in the hall, a few minutes ago," Mrs. Callahan said. "He's doing very well, and they're extremely grateful to you."

"Yeah, it was really brave," Patricia said, and grinned at her brother. "Incredibly *stupid*, but still really brave."

Gregory grinned back at her. "Are you mad that you couldn't go in, too, because of your arm?"

"I would have liked that better, yeah," Patricia admitted.

"Somehow, I don't think *I* would have liked it," their mother said. "Having one of you rushed to the Emergency Room is bad enough."

"Besides, she's already been once this week," Gregory pointed out.

Since there was no point in reminding her parents about *that*, Patricia decided to change the subject. "Hey, Dad, I forgot to tell you — I really like your new snow boots."

Mr. Callahan checked his feet, and saw his ancient pair of Mighty Mouse slippers. "Well, will you look at that."

"I've actually been trying *not* to look at them," Mrs. Callahan said, and they all laughed.

"You know what's funny?" Gregory asked. "This feels like a totally normal Christmas Eve for us."

His parents and Patricia laughed again — because that's *exactly* how it felt.

11

The mood in the treatment room was still cheerful, when a very young-looking resident doctor named Dr. Hammalah came into the room to examine Gregory's chart.

"Well, Greg, we're happy with the way you're doing, but I think you're going to be spending the night here," the doctor said.

Gregory stared at him. "Do I have to? I feel pretty okay now."

Dr. Hammalah shrugged. "Sorry, we need to keep an eye on you overnight. But we should be able to discharge you tomorrow morning."

Gregory didn't exactly look thrilled, but he didn't argue, either. "Can Santa Paws stay in my room, at least? To be, you know, pet therapy for *me*?"

"Oh, I don't think so, Greg. I'm sure the animal hospital will keep him overnight, too," Dr. Hammalah said.

Gregory blinked. *"Animal hospital?"*

When he heard that Santa Paws had been taken somewhere else, Gregory was so distressed that he refused to be admitted as a patient unless Patricia and Mr. Callahan promised to go over to Angell Memorial right away, make sure that Santa Paws was all right, and come back with a full report.

Patricia thought that was a good plan since, now that she knew Gregory was going to be fine, she also wanted to be able to see Santa Paws for herself. As she and her father left the Emergency Room, the Harrisons came with them. They were going to go back to their house for a while, and give Aunt Emily a chance to come down and visit. By now, Uncle Steve might have arrived from Oceanport, and he would want to know all of the latest details about Gregory's progress, too.

There were at least half a dozen reporters, and almost as many camera crews, waiting just outside the Emergency Room.

"That's the family," one of them said, and they all gathered around to see if the Callahans were going to be making any public statements.

"Is it true that Santa Paws is missing?" a writer from one of the city dailies asked.

Mr. Callahan shook his head. "He's not missing. He's just at — an undisclosed location."

Patricia almost laughed when she heard the

phrase "undisclosed location." Did her father have a press secretary character in his new book?

"We heard he's missing," the reporter insisted. "Are you sure you don't want to comment?"

"Quite sure," Mr. Callahan said. "Thanks. Enjoy the holiday, everyone."

Once they were in the car, Patricia automatically turned on the radio. The news station was also reporting that Santa Paws was missing, and broadcasting a city-wide appeal for citizens to assist in locating him.

"That's weird," Patricia said. "Wouldn't you think they'd have asked us, before they started publicizing it?"

Mr. Callahan nodded. "It must be a ratings thing. After all, today's a pretty slow news day."

That seemed perfectly logical, and so Patricia snapped the radio off.

There wasn't very much traffic, but Mr. Callahan still had to drive slowly because the roads were so treacherous. The animal hospital was located over in a section of Boston called Jamaica Plain, a few miles away. When he turned the car into the parking lot, they could see that another group of reporters and television vans were already there.

Patricia looked at her father uneasily. "You don't think — ?"

He shook his head. "No, of course not. Don't worry, they're just looking for a nice Christmas Eve feature story."

Patricia hoped that he was right, but the television vans made it seem as though something more compelling than a holiday report was happening. As they walked toward the entrance, all of the reporters started asking them questions about Santa Paws being missing, and did they think he would ever be found, and other equally grim speculations.

Inside the hospital, Mr. Callahan went up to the reception desk. There were a number of people already in the waiting room, some of them holding pets. Several assistants and technicians were behind the front counter, making phone calls and filling out paperwork.

"Hi, we're the Callahans," he said. "We came to see how our dog, Santa Paws, is doing. He was sent over here by mistake."

The room instantly got so quiet that Patricia and her father caught on to the horrible truth.

Santa Paws *was* missing!

The dog had spent the rest of his ride in the ambulance waiting for an opportunity to escape. These people might be trying to help him — usually the men and women who rode in the cars and trucks with sirens were very nice — but, what if they *weren't*? All he knew for sure was that they were taking him someplace unfamiliar, and that meant that he couldn't trust them.

Besides, Gregory was hurt! He needed the dog's help. The dog had to find him right away, and these people were bad for not letting him do it.

Every time the ambulance slowed down, the dog would tense his muscles, getting ready for action. But they usually only stopped briefly, and then kept going. Finally, he felt the ambulance turn a couple of times, and come to a complete halt. He moved his paws restlessly underneath the blankets, trying to contain his excitement.

"Oh, no," Mabel said. "The IV came loose." The tube and needle were swinging free, and she carefully picked them up, so that they wouldn't trip over them or stick themselves with the sharp point, by accident. Then she checked the dog's front leg to make sure that he wasn't bleeding in the spot where the needle had been. "Should we get another one started, or just take him inside?"

Victor shrugged. "Why don't we just go in? He looks so good, he might not even need one anymore."

A third EMT, Larry, who had been driving, got out to open the back doors for them. Normally, one paramedic drove, while the other one worked on the patient in the back, but they had wanted to give Santa Paws some extra attention, and kept two EMTs with him the entire time.

As the doors swung open and the cold winter air rushed in, Santa Paws got ready to make his move. But, just in case, he gave the breeze a good, long sniff, first. What if his family *was* at this strange place? Then it would be silly to run away. But the only thing he could smell was a place a little bit like the building where he would go to visit his friend, Dr. Kasanofsky, sometimes. Except that there seemed to be *lots* of animals here. Too many! He needed to be with his family, not with dogs and cats he didn't even know.

Larry and Mabel started to ease the gurney out of the ambulance, while Victor bent down to pick up the discarded supplies they had used. After every emergency run, paramedics always had a lot of cleaning up to do!

"Lie down, Santa Paws," Mabel said, as the dog started to ease himself to his feet. "We don't want you to fall off."

The dog didn't like it when anyone except for his family told him to lie down. He didn't even always like it when the Callahans told him! Having to lie down usually meant that someone thought he had been a bad dog. So he kept standing up, readying his legs to spring.

Then, before they could tell him to lie down again, he lunged forward and off the gurney. He landed in a pile of shoveled snow, and looked around nervously. No, he had definitely never been to this place before. Why had they taken him here? What did they want? He didn't like this *at all*.

Mabel and Larry looked at each other with alarm. It was easy to see that the dog was scared, and they didn't want to do anything to make him run away.

Larry bent down, holding out his hand. "Come here, Santa Paws," he coaxed. "It's okay, boy."

Santa Paws backed away slowly, paying attention to everything around him, just in case someone tried to come up to him from behind.

Larry and Mabel approached him from two different directions, hoping to cut off any chance he would be able to escape. The dog waited until they were almost close enough to grab him, and then he charged right past them, knocking Larry down on the way. He wasn't sure where to go — he didn't like scary, unfamiliar places! — so, he just ran toward the street.

All three paramedics raced after him, but the dog outdistanced them with no trouble whatsoever.

"Santa Paws, come back!" Mabel called.

The dog heard all three of them shouting out his name, but he tuned the voices out. Nothing around here looked — or smelled — familiar, and he was afraid that they might have taken him very, very far from his family. He slowed a little when he got to the busy street, not sure which way he should go. But now they were getting closer, and he didn't have much time to decide. He had to choose, and so he turned right.

He kept running as fast as he could, and left the paramedics far behind him.

Now all he had to do was find the Callahans!

Inside the animal hospital, the three paramedics explained what had happened — and didn't look either Patricia or Mr. Callahan in the eye once. They felt very guilty about not having been able to move more quickly, and stop Santa Paws from getting away.

Patricia let her father do all of the talking, because she wasn't sure if she was capable of answering graciously. How could they have lost Santa Paws? Especially when he didn't even feel well? On top of which, it was *Christmas Eve*. Shouldn't they have been more careful?

Once they had made their apologies, the paramedics left the building. They hurried to their ambulance, doing their best to avoid the press on the way. They had lost Boston's Hero — and they all felt miserable.

Standing in the middle of the main waiting room, Mr. Callahan let out his breath. "Thank you for not yelling at them, Patricia," he said. "They feel horrible enough about the whole thing as it is."

Patricia scowled. "All they had to *do* was bring

him along with us to Mass General, the way they should have."

Mr. Callahan nodded, and patted her good shoulder. "I know. But they thought they were doing the right thing, and — unfortunately, we all make mistakes."

Patricia knew that that was true, and she was actually blaming herself, for not making sure that the ambulance Santa Paws was in had been following Gregory's. But, at the time, she'd been so worried about her brother that she hadn't been paying close enough attention. She had just assumed that Santa Paws was right behind them.

Mr. Callahan went to talk to two of the veterinarians, and find out as much as he could about how Santa Paws might be feeling, and how far they could expect him to be able to travel on foot. The veterinarians had examined all of the paramedics' field notes, as well as some printouts of his heart rate. The good news was that they thought he was in surprisingly good shape physically, despite his time in the frozen water, but the bad news was that that meant he could already be at least a couple of miles away by now, and maybe even farther than that. Several of the hospital employees had already gone out to search for him, but none of them had had any luck so far.

Mr. Callahan left all four of the cell-phone

numbers, as well as their home number in Ocean-port and the Harrisons' number. That way, if anyone saw or heard *anything* about Santa Paws, they would have no trouble getting in touch with them.

When they walked out to the car, the reporters were unexpectedly considerate about not approaching them with intrusive questions, or taking photographs, or using their video-cameras to film them.

"Anything we can do to help?" one of them asked.

"It would be great if you could ask people to call the animal hospital, or the police, if they see him," Mr. Callahan said. "Thank you."

This was one situation when it might be *good* that Santa Paws was famous.

Before heading back to Mass General, Mr. Callahan and Patricia drove around the area for a while, to look for their dog. They circled the neighborhood, going up and down every possible street. Mr. Callahan also pulled the car over once in a while, and they would get out and call his name, in case he might hear them and come running. Unfortunately, they saw no signs of him whatsoever. To make matters worse, it was starting to get dark, and that would make searching even more difficult.

"I think we should head back to the hospital

now," Mr. Callahan said finally — and reluctantly.

Patricia was going to protest, but she just nodded.

"He's found his way back to us before," Mr. Callahan reminded her. "There's no reason why he can't do it again."

Patricia nodded, but the thought that they *might* get their dog back just wasn't very comforting.

By the time they returned to the hospital, Gregory and Mrs. Callahan had already heard the terrible news. Gregory had taken it very badly. He'd been lying curled up on his side ever since, refusing to talk to anyone.

Uncle Steve had arrived, and he was sitting next to Mrs. Callahan. Even wearing an ordinary ragg wool sweater and khaki pants, he still looked as though he was in uniform. But that made sense, since he'd spent his entire adult life in the army, and then as a police officer. Usually, he was fairly gung-ho and talkative, but under the unhappy circumstances, he just nodded hello at them and they nodded back.

"Why aren't you out there looking for him?" Gregory asked, his voice muffled by his pillow.

"We were, Greg," Mr. Callahan said. "But it's dark out there now, and — well, we just couldn't find him. Later, we'll go search all over the Harrisons' neighborhood, in case he tries to come back there."

Gregory slumped deeper into his pillow, while the rest of them sat there.

In silence.

The dog ran, and ran, and ran. Once he was finally sure that the strangers would never catch up to him, he stopped. It was time to try and figure out where he was — and how to get home!

He stood on a tall pile of snow, and raised his nose into the air. He could smell all sorts of city smells, but none of them were familiar. He was cold, very hungry, and felt like taking a nap. But finding his family mattered more than any of those things.

He sniffed repeatedly, but it still didn't help him solve the mystery of where he was. He had the brief sense that the Callahans were somewhere nearby, only then it was gone. So he sat down in the snow to think for a while. It was nice to rest his legs for a few minutes, too. In fact, he was so worn out that he decided to let himself take a little nap, after all. Then, when he woke up, he might be able to think of the best way to find the Callahans.

The dog dug himself a little nest in the snow and then crawled inside. The hole gave him some shelter from the wind, which was a relief. He was cold! But, he was even more tired, so he closed his eyes.

He had been asleep for about twenty minutes, when a loud squealing noise woke him up. Right after that, there was a huge crash.

"Help!" a voice screamed. "Help me! I'm trapped!"

12

The dog leaped to his feet. Someone needed him! He galloped in the direction of the screams, wondering what terrible thing might have happened this time. The noises had been very scary! What he found was a small sports car that had skidded on the ice and crashed into a telephone pole. The doors on each side were badly crushed and wouldn't open, and there was a woman still inside. She was banging against the closed windows, trying desperately to get out.

There was smoke pouring from the engine, and the dog could see the beginnings of small flames shooting out. He had no time to waste!

A few people had come running over to see what had caused all of that noise. But they were afraid to approach the car, because they thought it might blow up. So they kept their distance, and just hoped that the fire department would be able to arrive in time.

Out of nowhere, a dark shape streaked past them, heading directly for the burning car. The dog jumped up onto the hood and yelped. Ow! The metal was hot! Using all of his weight, he flung himself onto the already-cracked windshield. It caved in the rest of the way, and the dog was a little surprised to find himself sprawled in the front seat. The driver was even more surprised.

The smoke was getting thicker, and the dog reached out with his front paw until he located the woman. Then he grabbed her coat in his teeth and guided her toward the hole in the windshield. She climbed through the narrow opening, with Santa Paws pushing from behind. Then she rolled off the hood and down into the snow, coughing from the smoke.

The flames were higher now, and the dog felt a little nervous about jumping through them. But there were some shopping bags on the front seat, and he grabbed the handles with his teeth. Then, using the bags as a shield, he hurtled through the windshield over the leaping flames. He slid off the hood and fell into the snow right on top of the woman.

"Get away from there!" someone in the street was yelling at the top of his lungs. "Hurry! It's about to blow!"

The woman was a little bit dazed, from the combination of being in an unexpected crash and inhaling so much smoke. So the dog had to drag her away from the car, since she was too confused to get up and walk. Once he had pulled her about twenty feet away, some people took over for him and helped her to a safe position further down the block.

The dog stood still for a second, trying to remember what he had forgotten. The bags! He ran back to the car and snatched up the shopping bags with his teeth. Then he dashed off, just as the car's gasoline tank ignited!

The force of the explosion knocked Santa Paws down, but he was far enough away by then so that he didn't get hurt. So, he just picked himself up, shook the snow from his fur, and carried the bags over to the woman.

In the flickering light from the fiercely burning car, the woman saw the same large dog who had pulled her to safety trotting toward her.

"You saved my Christmas presents, too?" she asked incredulously. Then she reached out to pat him. Miraculously, she had not been seriously injured, other than a few bruises, but she would never have been able to make it out of the car in time by herself. "You're a really good dog."

The dog wagged his tail. He never got tired of being told *that*.

"You know, he actually looks like Santa Paws," a man standing nearby said, "don't you think?"

His wife shook her head. "That can't be Santa Paws — he's missing, remember?"

"He's not missing, if he's right here," the man said logically. Then he snapped his fingers. "Santa Paws! Come here, Santa Paws!"

Hearing his name, the dog wagged his tail harder. It was always nice when people were friendly to him. More people were calling his name now, and they seemed to want him to stay. That was *extra*-nice of them, but he didn't have any time to stop right now. So, with one last tail wag, he galloped down the street away from them.

He had to resume his search for the Callahans!

Back at the hospital, the family was still sitting together in Gregory's hospital room without talking much. For the most part, none of them could really think of anything to say that wouldn't make the rest of them feel worse. It was certainly one of the *least* festive Christmas Eves any of them could have imagined. Patricia and Uncle Steve went off for a couple of hours to search Beacon Hill and the other nearby streets, but they didn't have any luck. Aunt Emily had printed out some fancy signs on her parents' computer, which Patricia and Uncle Steve hung up all over the neighborhood. Everyone they ran into on the street was very concerned when they heard that Santa Paws had disappeared, and promised to keep an eye out for him.

"We should drive over to the animal hospital, and put signs all over *that* neighborhood," Patricia said.

Uncle Steve nodded. "That's a good idea. Maybe we can head over there in the morning."

"He must be looking for us, right? Do you think he'd try to find us here, at Mr. and Mrs. Harrison's house, or would he — " Patricia hated saying the words aloud, in case that might make them more likely to be true — "start trying to get all the way back to Oceanport?"

"I don't know, Patricia," Uncle Steve said honestly. "I called in to let the department know what was happening, and they promised to put out an alert to all of the neighboring jurisdictions, too. If anyone sees him, they'll — "

"Try to catch him, and he'll get nervous and run away from them," Patricia said, finishing the sentence for him.

Uncle Steve sighed, knowing that that was true. Since he had been stolen two Christmases earlier, Santa Paws had a tendency to be very wary of strangers. "Well, if he gets out that far, there's a good chance he'll run into someone he knows, and he's more likely to feel comfortable going with them."

Patricia nodded, although it made her feel sick to her stomach to think of Santa Paws traveling all those miles, and having to cross so many busy highways along the way. It was just too dangerous. "We have to keep checking the Public Garden," she said. "That's where he saw us last, so that's where I think he'll try to go."

At least she *hoped* that's what he would do.

The dog loped down a few more blocks before stopping to try and get his bearings. This city was confusing! The streets were so small, and they went in too many strange directions. He would feel as though he was going the right way, and then suddenly, the street would loop off somewhere, and everything would feel wrong again. It was very confusing!

His stomach was rumbling, and he thought sad thoughts about Milk-Bones and other delicious things to eat. Maybe he should tip a trash can over — that was usually a good place to find food. But tipping over trash cans was bad, and he didn't like to be bad, unless it was absolutely necessary.

It was completely dark outside now, and getting colder every minute. Many of the little houses and buildings he passed were lit up with Christmas lights, which made him feel very lonely. Sometimes, he could even hear people singing or laughing inside. If he was with his family right now, he knew they'd be having a happy time. They always had a happy time! He whined softly because he missed them so much and felt extremely sorry for himself.

The *last* time he had been lost, Abigail had been there to keep him company. He hadn't been sure that he wanted some trouble-making kitten with him, but she had come along, anyway. Now he thought about that time wistfully, because it was so much nicer to travel with a friend, instead of being by himself.

Where *were* the Callahans and his cat friends? Were they still at that house on the tall hill, with those two nice people and his new friend Becky? What if they had gone back to their *real* house, by the ocean? But, they would never leave him in this big, scary city by himself — would they? What if they did? What would he *do*? He would be so sad. Even sadder than he was right now!

The dog fussed and fretted and whimpered to himself as he ran along the dark streets. It was just terrible to be alone. If he found his family again, he never, *ever* wanted to go anyplace without them for the rest of his life.

He felt so sorry for himself that he wanted to lie down and take another nap. He wished that he could lie down right where he was, and bark and howl until the Callahans came to find him. He stopped running to give himself time to mull that plan over. Would it work? No, this was a very big city full of strangers, and it might be too hard for the Callahans to know where to look for him, even though they were very smart.

But he felt so dejected that he decided to lie down anyway. He picked a quiet corner next to a darkened store and stretched out in the snow. But, ow! That was too cold! So he moved into the store's doorway, where the snow had been shoveled to one side. That was a little bit more comfortable, and he rested his muzzle on his paws.

There weren't very many cars driving on the street in front of him, but sometimes people walked by, laughing and talking. One man was even walking a little spaniel mix, which barked threateningly at him. The dog moved further into the doorway, and was glad to see them keep going past him without stopping.

But when he saw some people pause, stare at him, and start walking straight toward him, he jumped up. He thought he might have heard them saying "Santa Paws," but he didn't want to wait around and find out. He would just find someplace else to take a little rest.

He ran for a few more blocks, and then stopped to forage for some food. He was so hungry that his stomach had started hurting. And he was thirsty, too! It was terrible. But then, he came across a box of discarded doughnuts, and that made him happy. The pastries were dry and stale, but they still tasted just fine to him. In fact, they were delicious!

He couldn't find any water, so he licked some icicles hanging from a wrought-iron fence. That didn't really satisfy his thirst, but it was better than nothing.

Feeling quite refreshed after his sugary snack, the dog moved into an easy trot. It was much better than flat-out running, because it wasn't as tiring and he could cover more ground. He was just starting to feel as though he was making some real progress, when he heard a small, unhappy crying sound.

He traced it to a dark alley, where a frightened Labrador puppy was sitting all by himself in a pile of snow. The puppy was wearing a collar and leash, so the dog knew that he must belong to someone. When he saw the huge German shepherd coming toward him, the puppy whimpered pathetically and rolled over onto his back to show that he couldn't *possibly* be any kind of threat.

The dog ignored that, and picked up the puppy's leash in his teeth. Then he tugged on the end and ushered the jittery puppy out to the sidewalk. Since the puppy must have an owner, the dog decided to look for help. If he could find someone nice, maybe the person would know where the puppy lived.

The puppy was not very good at walking on a leash, which annoyed the dog. The puppy kept trying to wander off, or even go out into the street! It was very bad. Whenever the puppy misbehaved, the dog would tug sharply on the leash to let him know that he was displeased. Soon, the puppy figured out that it was easier to obey, than it was to fight against the leash — or Santa Paws — and they made much faster progress.

Up on the corner, the dog could see a group of people in the middle of an urgent conversation. Maybe they would want to help him! He led the puppy over there, and barked once.

The group had actually been discussing where they should look for their neighbor's lost retriever puppy. The boy who owned the puppy had been taking him for a bedtime walk earlier, and the puppy had run away, so that he could chase a bird. The bird turned out to be a piece of paper blowing in the wind, but by the time the puppy realized that, he was already lost. So, he had retreated into the nearest dark alley to hide, because he was afraid to walk around at night by himself.

"Hey, look," someone said. "There's JoJo now!"

Hearing his name, the puppy yapped cheerfully. The boy who owned him came running over to scoop him up.

"Mom, he's back," the boy said with a huge grin on his face as he hugged his puppy. "Isn't it great?!"

Watching the reunion made the dog wish that

he could find *his* family that easily. What a lucky little puppy. The dog sighed, and turned to leave.

"Wait a minute," the boy's mother said. "Wasn't that Santa Paws? Quick, somebody grab him!"

Everyone turned to look, but it was too late — the dog was already gone.

As the evening wore on, the Callahans got several reports of Santa Paws sightings. Some were on the news, while others came in on direct calls from the police department. Unfortunately, the upshot of the stories was always the same — Santa Paws had been seen, but he ran away before anyone could catch him.

So far, he had apparently pulled a woman from the wreckage of a burning car, stopped two men from having a fist-fight when they were leaving a somewhat rowdy holiday party, summoned help for a girl who had fallen down the icy steps of her triple-decker house and broken her ankle, and even found a little boy's missing puppy hiding next to a Dumpster. The puppy's owner insisted that, in a matter of moments, Santa Paws had also managed to train the puppy to heel perfectly. And those were only the incidents that had been *confirmed*. The police said that they had been getting lots of calls, telling them — among other things — that Santa Paws had gotten thrown out of a bar in Roxbury for barking too much, that he had been seen boarding a train at South Station, and most memorably, that he was going to be the guest soloist at midnight mass that night at a church in Allston.

When their parents decided to go down to one of the hospital cafeterias to get a quick bite to eat, Gregory and Patricia were left alone together for the first time in hours. Gregory still wasn't very conversational, but now that, so far, Santa Paws seemed to be safe, he had at least been willing to sit up and watch television. He had also been plotting each confirmed sighting on a map of the city Uncle Steve had gone out and bought for him. If they traced his route, that might make it easier to figure out where he was going.

"How are you feeling?" Patricia asked, tentatively.

Gregory shrugged. "Tired, I guess." He studied the map. "You think he's trying to find us? It *looks* like he's coming this way."

"Unless he's actually on that train heading out of town," Patricia said.

Gregory cracked a smile. It was a small smile, but it was a smile. Then the smile faded. "Do you think he's going to be okay? And that we'll be able to find him? Maybe even tomorrow?"

Patricia gave the answer she knew her brother needed to hear.

"Absolutely," she said.

13

The dog had a very busy night. Every time he thought he might be making progress in his journey to find his family, something would happen to make him detour from his path. In the city, people seemed to stay up very, very late. And they kept getting into trouble, too!

He was on the run almost all night long. Somewhere along the way, he had passed an apartment building where there was a terrible smell of leaking gas. He knew that wasn't good, and he had to bark and bark, and hit the front door with his paws, until someone came out of his apartment to see what was going on. The dog was glad when the man smelled the gasoline, too, and they hurried through the whole building to make sure that everyone went outside away from the smell, where it would be safe. Then, as soon as the big trucks with the sirens came, the dog left.

Then, he helped a man who had lost his favorite pair of gloves in the snow. After that, he managed to jump in front of a woman who wasn't paying attention to where she was going and had almost walked in front of a speeding newspaper delivery van by accident. It just went on, and on, and *on*.

Most of the people he ran into seemed to know his name, and some of them even chased him! The dog didn't like having so many strangers telling him to "Come," and trying to grab him by the collar. It was much better when they just said hi, and waved to him, and he wasn't sure why they were all trying to make him obey, like he was a bad dog. It didn't make sense. But each time, he would just dodge out of their way, and run off before they could get too close to him.

It was early in the morning when the dog came upon the big Christmas tree in front of the very tall building. It was familiar! He had been here with Gregory and Patricia! Yay! He barked a few times to celebrate, and a man walking by said, "Thank you. Merry Christmas to you, too, pup."

Now that he knew where he was, the dog was so excited that he practically bounced his way through the snowdrifts. He would see his family soon! Everything would be okay again!

When he got to the Public Garden, which was the next place he remembered, he ran around the entire park twice, checking to see if Gregory and Patricia might be there. He was very disappointed not to see them, because he had thought they might have been waiting for him. But he could still smell a trace of their scents near the spot where he and Gregory had jumped into the water yesterday. Was it yesterday? Maybe. The dog was so tired that it was hard to remember anymore.

The dog never planned to *swim* in that water again, but that didn't mean that he couldn't drink some. It didn't taste very good, but it was better than nothing. But now he was hungry again, and there was no sign — or smell — of any food nearby.

Would his family come here soon? Should he stay and wait for them? Or should he go find the house up high on the hill? The dog couldn't make up his mind, and he paced along the side of the pond for a few minutes. Then he thought of something. He could do *both*. He could go to the house, and if they weren't there, he could come back here and wait for as long as it took. Yes! That was just right.

Happy to have such a good plan, the dog trotted toward the nearest street, wagging his tail every step of the way. He was standing on the corner, waiting for some cars to go by, when he found himself lifting his front paw and raising his nose in the air.

Something was wrong! He didn't know what it was yet, but he *was* sure of one thing.

There were people nearby who seriously needed his help!

Gregory had been released from the hospital bright and early that morning. Mrs. Callahan wanted him to spend the rest of the day resting, but Gregory insisted that he felt great and was ready to go out and look for Santa Paws right away. They compromised by agreeing that they would go back to the Harrisons' house for a quiet Christmas breakfast, first. After that, they would discuss what to do next.

Uncle Steve and Mr. Harrison had already been out twice that morning, searching, but they hadn't seen any sign of Santa Paws. But then, the police called with a whole new list of possible sightings, and Gregory got busy marking them on his map, so that they could try to follow the new trail.

There were lots of different reports, from all over downtown Boston. During the night, Santa Paws had apparently located a gas leak and evacuated an apartment building. He had also brought a small group of lonely homeless people to a church where they could find some holiday cheer — and warm shelter for the night. He had even chased down a pickpocket near the Sheraton Hotel. More and more people had been calling the police to report their various interactions with the heroic dog — and a surprising number of them even sounded plausible.

The rumor that Santa Paws had been seen running around the outfield at Fenway Park probably wasn't true.

Probably.

There wasn't much conversation at breakfast, but everyone tried to act as jolly as possible, so that Miranda and Lucy could enjoy the fact that it was Christmas and not have their holiday spoiled. Abigail was so unhappy about Santa Paws not being there, that Patricia held her on her lap during the entire meal to try and make her feel better. But even when she offered her a little bite of bacon, Abigail just sighed and turned her head away. Becky was lying in the front hall, near the door, moping, and Evelyn couldn't find enough energy to jump up on the Harrisons' kitchen counter and enjoy her usual mealtime view. She just sat in the corner, washing her face lethargically.

"Why does Santa Paws always go find the trouble at Christmas?" Miranda asked at the breakfast table.

Lucy chirped in with something that sounded either like "Doggie," or maybe "Daddy."

"I don't know, Miranda," Mr. Callahan answered. "I guess he just can't resist helping people, whenever he can."

"He should be *here*," Miranda said firmly. "It would be *much better*."

No one could disagree with that — so, no one did.

In the meantime, the dog had been busier than ever. The moment he had sensed trouble, he ran across Boston Common until he came to what looked like a building growing right up out of the ground. One of the doors was partway open, and he squirmed his way inside and ran down a long flight of stairs.

He found himself in a very strange place, with metal gates and tunnels and scary, loud machines rushing by. Except that all the machines were coming to a stop at once, with deafening, high shrieking sounds which hurt his ears. The doors on one of the machines near him slid open, and people came running out. The dog was so surprised that he actually jumped about a foot in the air. Then he decided that the machines must be *really* big cars. Too big, as far as he was concerned.

The people who had been on the machines were all yelling and pointing into one of the tunnels. The lights in the big place began to flicker, and the dog smelled burning electricity just as they all went out with a sudden crackling noise. Now it was so dark that people were bumping into each other and they seemed to be very frightened. After a minute, a couple of people came onto the platform holding powerful flashlights, but it was still very hard to see.

The dog decided that the people should all go outside in the fresh air. It was just too noisy in here with so many of them talking and shouting at once, and he didn't like it that they kept bumping into each other in the dark. Someone might get hurt that way! So he stood near the exit to the stairways and barked over and over.

Gradually, people filed in his direction, following the sound of his bark. He had learned how to herd during the many times he had rescued stray cows in Oceanport, so he ran from side to side, to make sure that they stayed in an orderly group. It wouldn't be good for any of them to get lost in the dark. Once he had guided them safely to the exits, they began rushing up the stairs and out of the building.

"You sure all the power's out, Bill?" one of the men with the flashlights was yelling. "I can't send anyone down there, if there's a chance the third rail might still be live."

"The whole grid's out," Bill answered. "They've lost power in the system all the way to Government Center and Copley. I don't know how bad the accident was, though — we can't get through to the conductor."

Now that most of the people had left the subway station, the dog moved toward the end of the platform. He sniffed the air in the tunnel, trying to figure out what was going on. He could hear panicked voices somewhere deep in the blackness, and it sounded like the people were stuck inside one of the big, metal machines. The dog was about to jump onto the tracks so that he could go rescue them when he heard a rumbling sound, inside the tunnel. Then, he heard bits of concrete crashing down, and a wave of dust blew up to obscure the entire platform.

Part of the subway tunnel had just collapsed!

After breakfast, Uncle Steve and Aunt Emily were going to take Miranda and Lucy to eleven o'clock Mass with the Harrisons. At the last minute, the Callahans decided to go along with them. It was Christmas, and attending church felt like the right thing to do. It was a very beautiful small cathedral, and once they got there, they were very glad that they had come. They were also touched when the entire congregation prayed for Santa Paws to return home safely.

When the Mass was over, the whole family went outside. It was a beautiful, sunny day, and some of the snow was starting to melt. The church was located at the base of Beacon Hill, so it was an easy walk over to the Public Garden. Of course, Lucy actually rode, since she was in her stroller.

Gregory and Patricia hadn't *really* expected

Santa Paws to be standing there magically inside the park, waiting for them — but they were still disappointed when they didn't see him. They had been hoping that, by some miracle, he would have gone to the place where they had been together last. By now, a day later, there were so many different tracks in the snow, both dog and human, that they couldn't even tell which ones were his, anymore! It was as though he had just been erased from their lives, and even though it was Christmas, more than anything, they both felt like crying.

There seemed to be a lot of commotion coming from the direction of Boston Common, and they could hear sirens, and see flashing lights everywhere.

"That doesn't look very good," Mrs. Callahan said. "I wonder what's going on?"

A couple walking by stopped.

"You didn't hear?" the man asked. "A train derailed between Park Street and Boylston, and I guess part of the tunnel caved in. One of the track switches shorted out or something. They've been down there rescuing people for the last hour now."

"I hope there weren't any injuries," Mrs. Harrison said with a worried look on her face.

The man shrugged. "I don't know. I hope not. But I sure saw a lot of ambulances and fire trucks and all."

That was sad news to hear on Christmas Day, and the adults — as well as Gregory and Patricia — knew better than to discuss it any further in front of Miranda and Lucy. Without having to talk about it first, they headed toward Pinckney Street, so that they could get the children home.

They were halfway across Beacon Street, when Patricia stopped.

"Wait a minute," she said.

They all looked at her.

"*Rescuing* people," she said. "For more than an *hour*."

They all exchanged glances. Could it be as easy as that? Would Santa Paws, just as Miranda had said earlier, have gone to "find the trouble"?

"Dad, can we at least walk over there?" Gregory asked. "We won't get in the way or anything. We can just — look."

Mr. Callahan looked at his wife, who made a gesture that was somewhere between a nod and a shrug.

"Why don't the two of us take the children up to the house," Mrs. Harrison said, gesturing toward her husband. "Then, the rest of you can catch up."

Predictably, Miranda wanted to "go with the grown-ups," instead of returning home, but Mr. Harrison distracted her by promising to watch *The Little Mermaid* with her, even though they had already seen it twice during the last three days. Miranda liked that idea, and happily went off with her little sister and grandparents.

Once they were out of earshot, Mrs. Callahan let out her breath.

"Please don't get your hopes up," she said to Gregory and Patricia. "We're just going to go have a quick look, to be sure."

Gregory and Patricia nodded, although they were already so excited that they barely heard her. They might actually have a chance to find their dog! After all, where *else* in the city would he be right now? It made perfect sense.

The entire area around the Park Street subway entrance had been blocked off, and only rescue workers were permitted to go inside. A big crowd of onlookers had gathered, anyway, standing as close to the barricades as possible. By listening to their conversations, and asking a few questions, the Callahans were able to get more details about the accident.

Apparently, there had been about sixty people on the subway train — which all Bostonians called "The T" — when the first two cars unexpectedly jumped off the tracks. The conductor did his best to stop the train from crashing, but it slammed directly into one of the main power grids. The force of the collision weakened the supports above it, and part of the tunnel caved in. Miraculously, no one had been killed, but at

162

least twenty-five people had been injured. Most of the injuries were things like wrenched backs, and minor concussions, but a few people had more serious problems like broken legs, or were having trouble breathing because there was so much dust in the tunnel.

Fortunately, there had been no electrical fire when the transformer shorted out, so the firefighters had mainly been rescuing the people trapped in the two front cars, and working to make sure that the rest of the tunnel was structurally sound before allowing the repair crews to go in.

"Man, you should have seen those K-9 teams," a college student with long hair and a patchy mustache said to Gregory and Patricia. "They must have been in and out of that tunnel at least ten times. It was excellent."

Gregory and Patricia each felt a flash of hope — followed by the disappointing thought that he must have meant that the only dogs here were professional search and rescue dogs. Then Gregory caught a glimpse of a tired police officer bending to give a bowl of water to a shepherd whose fur was covered with dust and soot.

"Hey, that's him!" he said. He ducked underneath the barricade, with Patricia right behind him. They ran toward the dog, ignoring all of the police officers ordering them to stop. Hearing their footsteps, the dog handler looked up — and so did her dog.

It wasn't Santa Paws. It was a different German shepherd, and up close, there was almost no resemblance at all.

"Go back behind the barricades, okay, kids?" the dog handler said. "We really want to keep this area clear."

"Sorry," Patricia said, more disappointed than she could ever remember feeling before. "We just thought — sorry, we made a mistake."

"Okay, people!" one of the fire officers in charge of the operation shouted through a bullhorn, sounding extremely happy. "We're all clear! Rescue 1's bringing up the last two right now. Nice work, people, we saved them all!"

Every single one of the rescue workers cheered, and the crowd behind the barricades began clapping and shouting congratulations. The doors to the subway station swung open and several grimy firefighters came out with the final two people who had been trapped in the front subway car. One of them was on a stretcher, and wearing an oxygen mask, but she was waving at everyone, so it was clear that she would be all right. The other victim was limping, but had a big smile on his face.

And, leading the way, wagging his tail triumphantly, was a large, confident, soot-covered dog. Gregory and Patricia stared at the dog for a second, and then began running toward him, calling his name.

This time, it *was* Santa Paws!

He raced over to meet them, barking joyfully and trying to jump on both of them at the same time. Gregory! Patricia! He had found them! Hooray!

Mr. and Mrs. Callahan hurried past the barricades, along with Uncle Steve and Aunt Emily, to join the jubilant celebration. The people behind the barricades began chanting "San-ta Paws! San-ta Paws!" over and over. Then, someone started a chorus of "We Wish You a Merry Christmas!" and everyone — including all of the rescue workers — started singing together.

"*Now* it feels like Christmas," Patricia said, and hugged Santa Paws for about the tenth time in the last two minutes.

"Hey, that is one fine dog you have there," a fire captain said to them with genuine admiration. "He had already brought about eight people out of the train before we even *got* here. And he did just great, working with the K-9 teams. Think he wants a full-time job?"

"I think he wants a Milk-Bone," Gregory said, laughing — and maybe even crying a little, at the same time. His parents and Patricia were doing the exact same thing, because they were so grateful to have their dog back, safe and sound.

The dog barked. Yes! He wanted a Milk-Bone!

He wanted some supper! He wanted to go play with Abigail and Evelyn, and his new friend Becky! He wanted to take a *really long* nap!

But, most of all, he wanted to be with the Callahans, who he loved so much. And now here they all were, together again!

This was going to be the best Christmas he had ever had!